*WES*
*OVE*

# THE OUTLAWS

# THE OUTLAWS

## Wayne D. Overholser

**GUNSMOKE**

First published in the US by Five Star

This hardback edition 2013
by AudioGO Ltd
by arrangement with
Golden West Literary Agency

ISBN 978 1 471 32116 0

**British Library Cataloguing in Publication Data available.**

Printed and bound in Great Britain by
MPG Books Group Limited

## Editor's Note

Although there are other Western stories that Wayne D. Overholser wrote during his career that have yet to appear in book form, having appeared only in various magazines, THE OUTLAWS was the last Western story he wrote before his death in 1996. It brings to a close a relationship with the reading public that began sixty years before with publication of the story, "Wanted Man," in *Popular Western* (12/36). Wayne D. Overholser remained his life long an author of the Western story who rarely disappoints with his narratives of characters about whom his readers come to care deeply and who confront the dire complexities of life on the American frontier in such a way that they embody universal themes of the human condition.

# Chapter One

My name is Del Delaney, a well-known name to most of the Montana sheriffs because it was on reward dodgers tacked to the walls of their offices. The hell of it was I hadn't done a damned thing to put it there. The charge was rape. It was the last crime in the book I'd ever commit.

I had ridden into Prairie City to go to the dance that they have the first Saturday of the month. It was always a big occasion. We were stuck up there close to the Canadian line all by ourselves, so we didn't have any entertainment we didn't figure out for ourselves.

I'd been riding for Wineglass for ten years. It was a fair-size outfit about ten miles from town. My mother taught the primary grades in the Prairie City school and cooked for Wineglass in the summers. She didn't care for dances, so I rode in alone and stopped at her house to clean up. I figured I'd sleep late Sunday morning and ride back to Wineglass in the afternoon, but it didn't work out that way.

A young woman named Ruby Prentiss was the cause of my trouble. I should have kept my distance from her, and I knew it, but she was like a magnet, being the prettiest woman in the county. She'd been married twice. The talk was that she'd slept with all the men who lived within fifty miles of town, but I never took much stock in those rumors. It was just that she was like a bright flower in a bunch of pale ones, so the men, like bees, were attracted to her. I was no different than the others.

When I walked into the dance hall, Ruby was surrounded by about ten men. She was flirting with all of them, a trick she had mastered when she was about ten years old. Then the unexpected happened. Ruby saw me, excused herself, and headed right for me, leaving the men who had surrounded her glaring at me. When she got to where I stood just inside the doorway, the orchestra started to play, and there wasn't anything to do but ask her to dance.

By the time the evening was over, I'd had about half the dances with Ruby, with the other men glaring harder at me than ever. It made me feel fine, particularly because the man who glared the hardest was Sid Blackwell, a deputy sheriff who had been going with Ruby. The first thing she told me was that she'd just broken up with Blackwell.

As far as I was concerned, Blackwell was the nearest thing to a complete zero I ever saw, and why Ruby put up with him was more than I could figure out. We were the same age, twenty-seven. We'd gone through school together, but we'd never been friends. In fact, I'd had more fights with him than all the other boys put together. He never could whip me, but he kept trying. Now that we were grown up, he still tried when he had an excuse, but he never got the job done.

When the dance was over, it seemed up to me to take Ruby home. At least she made it plain she expected it, so I obliged. Knowing that Ruby was poison didn't keep me away from her. I guess it's like anything that's on the forbidden side: it just seems too attractive to turn down. Besides, I got a lot of pleasure out of the way Sid was hating me with his eyes. I figured he'd jump me before the dance was over, but he didn't.

Ruby lived alone in a little cottage on the north end of Main Street. She snuggled up to me all the way to her house, hanging onto one arm and looking up at me as if I was the greatest thing on earth. It got to my head, I guess, thinking about Sid and the other men who'd give their right arm to be where I was.

I guess that Ruby had picked me to take Sid's place and be her steady. I'd gone with several girls, but I wasn't ready for marriage, or even going steady with anyone. I don't know yet what Ruby saw in me, if she saw anything. I was just another cowhand making my forty a month and beans. I had about a thousand dollars saved, and my mother had some money she was going to lend me. My boss had promised to help me start a little spread next to Wineglass, and I could work for him part time until I got my herd started. Still, I wasn't a prize catch, and Ruby wasn't the kind of woman who'd want to work hard enough to help a poor man start a ten-cow spread.

That's the truth of it. Ruby was a hunter. When she got well done with a man, she'd dump him as she always had and start looking for another one. All this didn't occur to me at the time. I still felt as if I were walking on air and that I was just about the biggest man in the State of Montana.

That feeling lasted until we got to her house and she invited me in. She pulled the blinds and locked the front door, then she came to me and kissed me. I've been kissed by a lot of girls, but none of them could kiss like Ruby Prentiss. Talk about fireworks going off and the earth rocking under your feet, well, it had never happened to me before. I understood then why the single men in Prairie City made fools of themselves over her.

She took my hand and led me into her bedroom, then she began taking off her clothes. I hadn't thought this through. All of a sudden I realized what I was into. That was when I got scared. Not that I objected to sleeping with her. I just figured she was trapping me. All of a sudden I had a mental picture of her having a baby and naming me, and I'd have to marry her. As much as Ruby Prentiss excited me, she was the last woman I wanted to marry.

She had her dress off and was sitting on the side of the bed taking off her shoes when she looked over her shoulder and gave me one of her come-on looks that she was good at.

"Hurry up, Del," she said. "Don't keep me waiting."

Right then I panicked. I whirled around and headed for the front door.

She yelled: "Del, what's the matter with you?"

I was so anxious to get out of there that I had trouble unlocking the door. She ran out of the bedroom with one shoe off. The last thing I heard was her angry: "You son-of-a-bitch."

I ran home. I wasn't in that much of a hurry, but I ran anyway. I went to bed, but I kept thinking of what I had missed, alternately cursing myself for being a fool because I'd turned down what would have been a hell of an interesting night, and then thankful because I'd got out when I had.

I didn't sleep much until daylight, then I passed out as if I'd been drugged. About nine o'clock someone started pounding on the front door. I lay there a while, wondering who was so anxious to see me and wishing he'd go away, but he didn't, so finally I got up and pulled on my pants, then walked into the front room, still too groggy to know what was going on.

I came out of it the instant I opened the door. There was Sid Blackwell with the meanest and most triumphant grin on his face I ever saw on a human being. He had a cocked gun in his hand, and he pointed it right at my brisket.

"You're under arrest for rape," Blackwell said. "Go get

your clothes on and we'll find a nice comfortable cell for you. Don't get no idea of making a break for it. I'd just as soon shoot you as not."

That was a statement I could believe. I backed across the room fighting for breath. If I'd had a chance to figure out the worst thing that could happen to me, I wouldn't have thought of this. Sweat was breaking out all over me. The first thing that entered my mind was that I wouldn't have a chance if it came to a trial. Blackwell's dad was the judge. That was how Sid had gotten his star. He had never done a thing to show he could handle the job. It was just that the old judge had a lot of pull.

Actually Sid wasn't very smart. His dad wasn't, either, but he looked and talked like a judge, so he'd been able to fool the people for the past ten years. He'd arrange it so Ruby's testimony would be believed. Women were scarce in our county, and, if they were so-called "good women," they were trusted. Maybe Ruby wasn't a "good woman," but she wasn't a soiled dove, either. If she testified, she'd tell the jury how I'd taken advantage of her, and she'd have the jurors crying like a bunch of kids.

Then another thought hit me. If I let Blackwell lock me up, I wouldn't have a chance of getting out, and I'd wind up in Deer Lodge. I knew I'd go crazy if that happened.

"I didn't rape her," I said.

Blackwell laughed. It was just as mean a laugh as his grin had been. He said: "I ain't no judge or jury, but, if I was, I'd believe Ruby and I wouldn't believe a damn' word you'd say." He motioned toward the bedroom. "Get a move on."

I walked slowly into the bedroom, a dozen ideas about how to get out of this running through my mind, but none was any good. One thing I knew. I'd as soon have Blackwell plug me as do a stretch in the pen if I had my druthers. I'd talked to cowboys who'd been sent up for rustling, and, the way they told it, a man was better off dead than in prison.

I pulled on my shirt and buttoned it. I sat down on the edge of the bed and tugged on my boots. Then I ran a hand through my hair. All the time panic was getting hold of me. Somehow I had to get the jump on Blackwell and make a run for it. Sure, folks would say that was an admission of guilt, but the way I saw it, I didn't have a chance this way, so it didn't make much difference.

"You know, Del," Blackwell said smugly, "I've been dreaming about something like this for a long time. With Ruby telling how you tore off her clothes and carried her into the bedroom, and Pappy sitting up there in the judge's chair, you'll be lucky if they don't hang you."

I couldn't argue with that. I got up, saying—"I'm going to wash my face."—and started toward the bedroom door.

"Wear it dirty," he said impatiently.

"My eyes are gummed shut," I said. "You're not in that big a hurry to lock me up."

He backed into the living room. Like I said, he wasn't very smart. He was likewise stubborn. He said: "I'm in a hell of a hurry to lock you up. There's water in the jail. Wash when you get there."

"I'm gonna wash my face," I said. "You can shoot me in the back if you want to."

He didn't quite know what to do. Even Sid Blackwell wasn't stupid enough to shoot a man in the back, and that threw him into enough mental confusion to make him hesitate before doing anything. I knew it was the best chance I'd have. I took a few more steps toward the kitchen door, bringing me close to him, close enough to make a quick swipe with my left hand and knock his gun barrel down.

He pulled the trigger. The sound of the shot was like the

blast of a cannon in the small room. The bullet slapped into the floor beneath his feet. The next instant I brought my right fist through to his jaw. It was the best punch I ever threw in my life. I was still scared, and I knew it was my only chance, so I guess I gave it a little extra. Anyhow, my fist made a solid sound as it connected, and Blackwell went down in a pile. My hand hurt, but I didn't care about that.

Grabbing him by his feet, I dragged him into the bedroom. I tied his hands and feet and shoved a wadded-up rag into his mouth, then tied another rag around his face so he couldn't spit the gag out. He'd get loose eventually. If he starved to death, I wouldn't care, feeling the way I did right then.

I buckled on my gun belt and left the bedroom. A neighbor poked his head in through the door. He asked: "I heard a shot. Anything wrong?"

My heart missed a few beats, but I said, trying to make my voice normal: "No, I'm just awkward. My gun went off while I was cleaning it. Didn't hurt anything."

"You're lucky," he said. "Some jaspers shoot themselves in the foot that way."

"Yeah, I guess so," I said.

He left, and I went into the kitchen where I filled a flour sack with bacon, coffee, flour, sugar, and whatever I could find. Mom hadn't been home for several weeks, so there wasn't anything cooked I could pick up.

Then I did something I was sorry I had to do, but I had to have some money. She had been dropping spare coins and greenbacks into a sugar bowl, saving for a new heating stove for the front room. I took it all, so with what I had in my pants pocket I had about forty dollars. I never gave a thought of going to the bank and taking out what I had deposited there. All I could think of was getting out of town.

13

I wrote a note telling Mom not to worry, that I'd pay her back someday, then went into the front room and took a Winchester off an antler rack. It had been my dad's. Mine was out at Wineglass, and I wasn't going there to get it.

I closed the front door, then ran out through the back to the barn where Jim Dandy, my buckskin horse, was stabled. I saddled up and left town, riding north as if I was headed for Wineglass, but, as soon as I was out of sight of town, I turned and started angling southwest and put Jim Dandy into a gallop.

# Chapter Two

I kept riding in the same general direction, finally crossing the state line into Wyoming. I felt better then, thinking there was less chance a Wyoming sheriff would be interested in me than a Montana law man. I avoided the bigger towns, especially the county seats. On occasion I killed enough game to live on, but most of the time I stopped at country stores and bought supplies.

It was late spring, and I hit rain and occasional snow, and at times I was cold and uncomfortable, but all the time I'd tell myself that it was better than living in a cell in the Deer Lodge pen, and I was glad to exchange comfort for freedom. But all this time I had plenty of opportunity to think and view my future. It didn't look bright.

The timing of events has always interested me. Too, I've often wondered how life would have gone if someone else hadn't been at a certain place and a certain time. For instance, suppose I hadn't gone to the dance that night? Or suppose Ruby hadn't gone? Or suppose I had gone to bed with her? All this was idle speculation. Then I started asking myself why had Ruby accused me?

I guess I spent more time kicking that question around in my head than anything else. Sure, she was sore because I walked out on her. Chances are that had never happened before, so her pride was hurt, but another idea kept nudging my mind. Sid Blackwell had hated me ever since we'd been in the first grade, and for no reason I knew of except that I was always better at anything we tried than he was.

The harder he tried to top me, the worse anything turned out for him. It even got so I'd take his girls away from him. I guess I got some satisfaction out of it. Not that I was proud of myself. Mostly it was just the way things turned out. I never had tried to take Ruby because I'd always been gun shy with her, so he didn't have that to hate me for. But then, maybe he did have good and sufficient reason to hate me. I guess any man gets tired of playing second fiddle all the time.

Out of this speculation a new idea struck me. Blackwell might have put Ruby up to the whole thing. If I'd gone to bed with her and she'd yelled for help and Blackwell had been outside waiting for her to yell, and if she'd torn her clothes and said I did it, well, I'd have been worse off than I was now. It could have been a game set up from the beginning, with Blackwell paying her to trap me. Maybe they hadn't broken up at all. Anyway I cut it, it looked to me as if he'd finally won. I was on the run, and I didn't see how or when I could stop.

Many times I'd thought about striking out to see the country, but it had taken this sudden and violent situation to get me started. All I could do was stop somewhere and get a job and ride on before the law caught up with me. I'd met a lot of saddle tramps who operated that way. It would be fun for a while, but it wasn't my idea of an ideal life. Sooner or later I'd want to go home and see my mother, or maybe I'd decide that northern Montana was the best place in the world to live, and I'd go back. Maybe in time the law would forget it wanted me.

I didn't come to any conclusion. I'd just have to wait it out. I did for a while, then I just plain ran out of money. I drifted into Star Valley on the Wyoming-Idaho line and caught on with a Mormon outfit that was more farm than ranch. I had a pleasant enough situation except that I had to learn to do things I'd never done before. Plowing, for instance. While I was hanging onto the plunging handles of the plow, I began to get angry. I was branded as an outlaw, so why not be one? The notion was downright interesting. Plenty of good men had turned outlaw for that very reason.

My ride south had given me a pretty good idea of how an outlaw had to live. I'd been cold and hungry and tired, and I'd got used to looking back over my shoulder to see if anybody was chasing me. It would be a hell of a life and no mistake, but what other kind of a life was ahead for me? Go home and face the music? No, I couldn't do that, and it wasn't likely the case would ever be dropped as long as Sid was a deputy and his dad was judge.

I hung on in Star Valley for a month, but, when the boss's wife wanted me to hoe her garden, I decided it was too much, so I drew my time and struck out again, still heading south. If I was going to take the Owlhoot Trail, I figured that holding up a bank was the best way to start.

I'd thought about robbing some of the small stores where I'd stopped to buy supplies, but I figured there wouldn't be enough money in their safes to make it worthwhile. Besides, I felt sorry for those men. They never made much money, and they had families to support.

Then another thought struck me. Maybe I wasn't mean enough to be an outlaw. That notion upset me. Well, there was only one way to find out. The trouble was that after I'd done the job and found out how mean I was, it would be too late. Once the first bank had been robbed, there would be no turning back, but maybe there was no turning back now.

I'd heard of the town of Baggs a long time before I left Prairie City, so I headed for it. A couple of Wineglass riders had lived there, and they said it was a town where nobody asked questions. The Baggs businessmen liked outlaw money too well to quiz into a man's background.

Baggs was on the Colorado-Wyoming line, they'd said, and had been a hangout for the Wild Bunch. It wasn't far from Brown's Hole, so when Cassidy and his pals wanted to turn their wolves loose, they rode into Baggs. When they pulled out a day or so later, their purses were lighter, and the Baggs businessmen were that much richer. Robbing a bank was more than a one-man job, so I figured I might run into some outfit that needed another man.

I rode into Baggs about four o'clock on a bright afternoon in late May. It wasn't much of a town, but then I hadn't expected much. I turned into the first livery stable I saw and then got a room in the only hotel in town. I hadn't eaten since morning, so I stepped into the dining room for supper.

Two men were eating at a table near the windows that looked out on Main Street. One of them was a kid, about eighteen or twenty I judged, thin, small-boned, and not more than five feet, six. He had a very thin mustache, the kind a boy grows who's trying too hard to be a man; the other man was tall, six feet, two or better, and very skinny.

The kid looked up when I came in and motioned to me. "Ain't much fun sitting by yourself," he said. "This table's big enough for the three of us."

It was a friendly gesture, and I appreciated it. I said: "Thanks. You're right about eating alone." I held out my hand. "I'm Del."

He shook hands as he said: "They call me the Kid." He nodded at the older man. "He's John Smith."

I shook hands as I said: "I've met a lot of your namesakes."

He smiled wryly as he said: "There are a lot of 'em, all right. It's even the real name of some of 'em"

He was a sober man who looked as if he belonged behind the counter in a men's clothing store or in a bank counting out the day's receipts, but here he was, wearing cowboy duds and carrying a gun. The Kid was different. He was the bubbly, outgoing kind of person who considers every stranger a friend, but, after I'd sat down and given my order, I sensed something else about him. I wasn't sure, and I realized I might be making too quick a judgment, but I had a notion that back of his pleasant affability he was as deadly as a rattlesnake.

After a few minutes of conversation I gathered that Smith came from a little town in the Idaho panhandle and the Kid from a cowtown in eastern Oregon. They had been here a couple of days and were headed up the Little Snake in the morning to work for a cattle outfit, the biggest in the country according to the Kid.

I liked both of them. Maybe it was because I'd been alone too long. Even when I'd been working for the Mormon family in Star Valley, I'd felt alone. Not that they weren't friendly. I just didn't belong, mostly, I think, because they made a good deal of their religion and I was an outsider who just didn't believe the way they did. Before that I'd been alone all the way from Prairie City, so alone and jumpy I was afraid to talk to the store men from whom I was buying supplies.

I didn't feel that way about these men. I figured they were on the dodge, too. We talked, but not about anything important, just the weather, the country, the price of beef that had been going down all winter. They rose when they finished eating, the Kid saying: "This is a tough town, Del. It won't take you long to figure that out. It's my guess half the men you see around here are on the run."

They headed for the door, then Smith turned to call back: "Stop in at the Long Horn for a drink if you're not in a hurry to go to bed."

"Thanks," I said. "I'll do that."

I walked the length of Main Street after I'd eaten. It didn't take long. There weren't more than two hundred people in the town, I guessed. I passed some small office buildings that housed a doctor, a lawyer, and a real estate man, a number of bigger buildings that included the hotel, three saloons, two livery stables, a bank, a blacksmith shop, and a school. I didn't count them, but I don't suppose there were more than twenty houses scattered on both ends of the business block and a few on the side.

I came to a street that ran east and west, cutting at a ninety degree angle across Main Street. Colorado lay to the south, or so a sign said. Fair-size mountains were visible to the east, with a road running out through the sage brush until it was lost in the distance. There was nothing to the west, either, except miles and miles of sage brush covering the slightly rolling land, with here and there a butte sticking up from what was more or less a flat plain.

Somewhere out there to the west would be Brown's Hole, and I wondered if this was the way the Wild Bunch had come to town when Cassidy and his friends had ridden in on one of their sprees. I found myself wishing I had been here a few years earlier. I would have liked to have seen Cassidy and the Sundance Kid and the rest of them.

I stepped into the Long Horn after I'd seen the town. A dozen or more men were in the saloon: four playing poker, seven or eight strung out along the bar, and the Kid and John Smith at a back table, a bottle in front of them. The Kid motioned for me to come to their table, and I did.

"Sit down," the Kid said when I came up. "The bottle's half full."

"No, it ain't," John Smith corrected. "It's half empty."

"There you go again," the Kid said in an aggrieved tone. "Always taking the opposite side to what I say."

"Hell, all you've got to do is to look," Smith said. "You can see the top half is gone."

The Kid grinned at me. "Well, there's plenty."

"I'll get a glass," I said, and walked to the bar.

I stepped in between two cowboys who were drinking. They'd had enough, but they didn't know it. I glanced at them, thinking that about one more drink and they'd be on the floor. The bartender was waiting on a drummer at the far end of the mahogany, and I guess he was having trouble finding what the man wanted because he kept hunting through the bottles behind the bar and not having any luck.

I couldn't do anything but wait which was all right because I wasn't in a hurry, but the drummer was getting impatient, saying loudly that he guessed that he'd come to the wrong saloon. I wasn't aware that another man had come in, but suddenly he bulled his way up to the bar and rammed his elbows out on both sides of him as if he didn't have enough room. His right elbow caught me in the ribs and jolted me over a couple of steps and knocked the air out of my lungs.

I have an explosive temper, but usually I keep it under control. I didn't this time. This was the kind of thing that turned it loose. There simply was no excuse for what the man had done. He had plenty of room at the bar and didn't have to pick this particular spot.

It took a few seconds for me to regain my wind while the man hammered on the bar for service. Little red lights were dancing across my eyes. I've never been able to think clearly at such times; I act and think later, and that was exactly what I did then. I drew my gun and turned on the man and hit him across the top of the head with the barrel. He toppled forward, hitting his head on the bar, then slid to the floor and lay with his face against the brass foot rail.

I holstered my gun, suddenly aware that no one was saying anything, no one was moving. All of a sudden everyone except me was in a sort of trance, eyes fixed on the man on the floor, then the bartender took a long breath that made a strange, sighing sound, and he said in a low, awe-struck voice: "I'll be damned."

Then I was aware that the Kid was on one side of me, holding my right arm, John Smith on the other side, holding my left arm. The Kid said: "Let's move."

"Come on, bucko," Smith said. "Let's mosey out of here. Don't argue if you want to live to be an old man."

Ordinarily I would have given him plenty of argument, but suddenly the scene took on a nightmarish flavor. This was happening, all right, but I didn't seem to be a part of it. I was standing motionless, watching a crazy scene of frozen men, an unconscious man on the floor, and two new friends holding my arms and urging me to get out of the saloon. There was something in their voices that I belatedly became aware of, an urgency I hadn't heard before.

I took Smith's advice and didn't argue. We strode out of the saloon, the Kid saying: "We'll get our horses and slope out of here. We wasted our money getting a hotel room."

"Would you mind if I go up to my room and . . . ?" I began.

"Yes, we'd mind," Smith said. "We're riding."

In a matter of minutes we were out of town, headed east, a plume of dust rising behind us, and I still didn't know why we were in such a hurry.

# Chapter Three

We didn't ride far. We'd gone about three miles when the Kid motioned for us to turn off the road toward the Little Snake. We rode through a thick patch of cottonwoods to the north bank of the river and dismounted. We off-saddled and staked our horses out, then the Kid sprawled on his back in the grass and stretched.

"We won't build a fire," the Kid said. "I don't think old Bull will come looking for us, but, just in case he does, there ain't no sense in pointing to where we're at."

I'd held my feelings as long as I could. I said: "Damn it, I'm a big boy. How come I'm being nurse-maided like this?"

"Because you didn't have no better sense than to bend your gun barrel over Bull Hammer's head," the Kid said irritably. "Or maybe you never heard of Bull Hammer?"

"No, I haven't," I said.

The Kid sat up and stared at me, then at Smith. "Hear that, John. He never heard of Bull Hammer."

Smith nodded, his face as grave as usual. "I heard, but I'm not surprised. I don't remember hearing about him till we got to Rawlins."

The Kid pointed a skinny forefinger at me. "If you want to know why we played nurse-maid to you, I'll tell you. Bull Hammer is the meanest, toughest, orneriest son-of-a-bitch who ever pinned on a star. He's a killer who gets away with it because he's the law. Nobody bucks him, and it's a sure thing that nobody cracks him over the head with a gun barrel."

That didn't set right with me, and I shook my head. "I don't back off from nobody just because he wears a star," I said.

The Kid lay back in the grass. "All right, go back to Baggs and tell him you're the jasper that cracked him on the noggin and see what happens."

"I wouldn't do that was I you," Smith said. "Maybe we didn't have any right to interfere, but we kind of liked you, and we figured you didn't know how it was. You see, Hammer is *the* law. He's the Baggs town marshal and he's a deputy in the counties on both sides of the state line. Even back before Cassidy's day there was some rustling and horse stealing in these parts. Finally the cowmen got tired of it and hired Hammer to come in and stop it. He's a killer, both with his gun and with his fists. Now folks are saddled with him, and I'm not sure that's any better than having your cows rustled."

The Kid sat up and pointed his forefinger at me again. He said: "We ain't been in these parts very long, but we've seen him kill two men since we rode in. No reason, either, that we could see, though we heard later that one of the men had beaten him in a poker game and the other fellow stole his woman."

I sat down on the bank and stared at the water. I've never been one to start a fight, but I've never been a man to run away from one, either. I always figured I could take care of myself with either my fists or my gun, if I had to. I hadn't got much of a look at this Bull Hammer. I just knew he was bigger than I was by thirty pounds or more, but I've whipped bigger men than that. Still, I hadn't known what a tough *hombre* he was, or I'd have put a lock on my temper.

One thing was sure. The Kid and Smith thought they were saving my hide by getting me out of the saloon. Maybe they had, so I said: "I guess I owe you some thanks."

Then I remembered how still the saloon had become with everybody staring at Hammer as if they couldn't believe what they'd just seen. Then I knew damned well I owed them a whole pile of thanks. Bull Hammer must be as big and tough and mean as the Kid and Smith thought he was, or the men in the saloon wouldn't have reacted the way they had.

I said again: "Thanks. I don't want to die yet."

"That's better," the Kid said as he lay back once more in the grass. "Looked for a while there that you were sore because we done you a favor. That didn't smell like gratitude to me. I appreciate it if anybody saves my life. John here's done it a couple of times, and I owe him for it."

He was currying me down, and I didn't like it. He was a pushy kid, I thought. He'd left home too early, and he'd had to work too hard in a world of men to be accepted as a man. I had to fight an impulse to snap at him, but I kept my mouth shut. In a way he was right. I guess I just didn't want to be reminded of it.

"We'll mosey on to the J Bar in the morning," Smith said. "If we get there early enough, maybe we can get some breakfast."

"I'll be hungry by then," the Kid said. "Might as well come with us, Del. Maybe they'll have jobs for three men."

"Sure," I said. "Nobody's waiting anywhere for me."

We rolled in as soon as it got dark, but I didn't sleep for a while. I kept thinking about Bull Hammer and wondering how big and mean and tough he really was. Maybe I should go back to Baggs and find out.

I knew that was stupid thinking. I was lucky to be here and have both eyes and not have my balls kicked to pieces. I guess I just didn't see much reason for living. It was the same problem that had plagued me on the way down here. I just couldn't see much future for me.

Home meant more to me than I had ever thought it did, and now I couldn't go home. All I could see ahead of me was drifting from one riding job to another and winding up an old man, a saddle bum scrounging meals off whatever ranch I happened to wind up at. No, that life wasn't for me. If Bull Hammer had killed me, he might have done me a favor.

I finally fell asleep and dreamed about a big man with a face like a bull. He was charging me, and I couldn't get out of his way. I woke up just as he was about to gore me and discovered that Smith was awake and kneeling at the edge of the river to wash his face. I was surprised to see that it was dawn.

By the time Smith rose and turned, I was on my feet. He nodded in his grave way and said: "Good morning. I was kind of worried about you, faunching around the way you were. You must have had a bad nightmare."

"Yeah, I guess I did," I said, and let it go at that, not wanting to tell him that Bull Hammer had become a part of my dream world.

Smith toed the Kid awake as he said: "Time to rise and shine if you want breakfast."

The Kid stretched and yawned and finally sat up. He got his eyes open enough to stagger to the river and slosh water over his face. We saddled up and rode another three miles or so to the east until we came to the J Bar, the buildings set on a ridge overlooking the river.

The main house was a poor excuse, more of a shack than anything else. There was a good log barn and a maze of corrals, all well-kept, with ten or fifteen horses in the corrals next to the barn. I guessed that no women were around, that the owner took good care of his horses and didn't give a damn about the house he lived in.

Just as we were tying in front of the bunkhouse, men began pouring out through the door and heading for the cook shack. None of them seemed to notice us until the last man appeared. He stopped and shook hands with us.

"We fetched a friend along," Smith said, nodding at me. "We were hoping you might be able to use him, too." Smith motioned to the man who had just shaken hands with him. "Del, this is Stub Rawls. He ramrods this outfit."

Rawls was a squat man with pale blue eyes and a firm handshake. I would have been disappointed if he'd said he couldn't give me a job. He looked me over, chewed on his lower lip a moment, then he said: "You look like you'll do. The boss ain't here, but you've got a job till he says otherwise."

"Thanks," I said. "I haven't been eating real regular lately, so I'd appreciate a chance to work."

He turned toward the cook shack, saying it was time to put on the feedbag. The rest of the crew was about what I expected, mostly young cowboys, and not a tough hand among them, if I read them right. I had a hunch they were largely drifters and maybe on the dodge like me and the Kid and Smith. They were friendly enough, and none of them struck me as bullies, the kind you have to whip or ride a killer horse to be able to work with them.

We had showed up just at the right time because Rawls put us to work shoving a good-size herd of two-year-olds off the bottomland near the river toward the high country to the east. Stub allowed they'd had a tough winter and the grass was slow coming up in the mountains. I could see that the bottomland had been badly overgrazed and the move to the mountains had been slow in coming.

I was curious about who owned the J Bar, but Rawls

didn't say who he was. The men didn't, either. Three weeks went by, and finally I asked Smith and the Kid if they'd heard anything about the owner.

"Not a damn' thing," the Kid said. "Stub rode into Baggs and hired us. Just said they was short-handed for the summer and the job would last until fall roundup. That suited me fine."

"I'm a little bit like you, Del," Smith said. "I've got a hunch there's something funny about this operation, but I don't know what it is."

"I don't see nothing funny," the Kid said. "A man who owns an outfit like this must have plenty of *dinero,* so he's probably in Cheyenne or Denver sleeping with purty women and making up for a long winter."

"Maybe," Smith said, "but I don't believe it. I've got a hunch something's not right here."

"Aw, you and your hunches," the Kid scoffed. "You're scared of ghosts, too."

"Sure," Smith agreed, winking at me. "You've never seen a ghost."

"No, and I never will," the Kid snapped.

I wasn't given to hunches, but I didn't like the situation. I wasn't sure why except that a few hints were dropped by some of the men that sounded a little scary to me. For instance, I heard one of them say the horsemen would be coming in before long and maybe it would be time to move on. I didn't know what that meant, and, since I wasn't part of the conversation, I didn't ask.

By the end of the fourth week I was convinced that every man here except Rawls was on the dodge and he might wake up some morning and find his crew gone. I never asked the Kid or Smith why they were here, but it finally came out.

One day, when we were hazing a dozen steers back from the river that was the J Bar's south boundary, the Kid said that he had killed a man. I wasn't sure from the way he told it whether he had intended to kill the fellow or not. Apparently it happened during some horsing around when they were pretending to shoot at each other. I was inclined to think he did intend to shoot the man because there was a lot of hard feelings on the Kid's part. The other cowboy was bigger and stronger and was a bully who had taken advantage of his size and strength to abuse the Kid, all the time pretending it was fun.

Anyhow, the Kid figured the sheriff wouldn't consider it had been in fun, so he lit out as soon as it happened and had been running ever since. I caught a glimpse of that insight I'd had the first time I'd met the Kid, that beneath the veneer of friendliness he was a very dangerous man who was capable of killing.

The Kid was silent for a long time after he had told me that, thinking back over what had happened, I guess, then he burst out: "I'm glad I killed the son-of-a-bitch, but it was different with John. He killed a man he caught in bed with his wife. He's sorry about the whole business. The man had been his boss in a bank he worked for and he liked the bastard, but, when he saw 'em naked in bed together, he got his gun and shot the ornery son before he could get out of the house."

I told myself that explained the grave, even sad expression I had so often seen on the man's face. I had never known him to laugh. As a matter of fact, he seldom even smiled. "I don't think a jury would have found him guilty," I said.

The Kid nodded. "That's what he says, but he just didn't want to go through a trial and drag his wife through it. You know, he still loves that woman. I don't see how he can, but he does." He looked at me and said directly: "What put you on the run?"

"How do you know that I was?" I asked.

"Just a guess."

I told him, and he grinned. "Now that is a hell of a note. I had trouble with a woman in Rawlins. John said there was no fury like that of a rejected woman or something like that. I guess that's what hit you."

"I reckon," I said, and didn't tell him that I had a hunch Sid Blackwell was behind my trouble.

I asked the Kid how long he figured on working here, and he shrugged his shoulders and said as long as nothing popped up to change things. It did. That evening the boss and four other men rode in bringing about twenty of the finest-looking horses I ever saw in my life. The horsemen, I thought, had arrived.

# Chapter Four

The boss was named Jerry Sewell. I didn't like him worth a damn. Maybe it was because he didn't pay any attention to me or the Kid or Smith. As far as he was concerned, we had been working on the J Bar for years. In fact, he didn't pay much attention to any of the crew. I soon came to the conclusion that he didn't know and didn't care who had been here before and who hadn't, and that Stub Rawls could do what he pleased when it came to hiring and firing, and maybe even to buying and selling.

Sewell was a hardcase, and so were the four men who had helped bring the horses in. Sewell was a lanky man with dark eyes that seemed to be nervously shuttling around from one thing to another, seldom focusing on anything very long. Maybe he had learned this from being on the run most of his life. I didn't know that he'd been on the run or was now, but the thought occurred to me.

All five were dressed in black from their boots to their Stetsons, and they rode black horses. I wondered about that, but I didn't mention it to anybody for a while. The five ate supper with us, but sat apart at the end of the long table as if we didn't really belong together. None of them, including Sewell, talked to us except for a few words passed with Rawls.

As soon as the meal was finished, Sewell led the way to the corrals where they had penned the new horses. They stood talking, motioning, and sometimes pointing to one of the horses. The rest of us hunkered down in front of the bunkhouse and smoked. Nobody said anything. We just watched Sewell and the others, but none of us tried to join them.

I was uneasy about the whole business and I sensed that the others were, too. I'd felt at home from the morning I'd ridden in here, but I didn't, now. I remembered what one of the men had said about it being time to move on when the horsemen rode in. I looked at the Kid and then at Smith, who gave me a small grin, and I had a hunch that they were thinking the same thing.

After half an hour or so Sewell and the other four headed for the main house. I guess they went to bed because none of them showed up later in the bunkhouse. The others except Rawls got up and strolled away in groups of two or three.

"Stub," I asked, "what in hell is going on?"

He didn't answer for a few seconds, then he flipped his cigarette away. "Oh, nothing. It's always this way when the boss shows up. He don't care much about what happens here as long as it don't cost him nothing. He's more interested in horses than he is in cows."

That struck me as peculiar because he had too many cattle to overlook. I mean, they represented a chunk of money. But maybe that didn't cut much ice with him. Some men liked horses and didn't care for cows just like some men couldn't stand sheep.

I was going to let it go at that, but the Kid wouldn't. He blurted out: "Don't make no sense, Stub. This is a good spread. You've got a good crew. The grass is a mite slow this summer, but it's coming. You'll have a fair-size herd to sell come fall. There's something damned funny about this whole lay-out." He swallowed, and added: "Them jaspers including the boss act like we ain't as good as they are."

Rawls took paper and tobacco out of his pocket and shaped up a cigarette. He said: "Well, Kid, I guess there's a lot of things in this old world that don't make sense. This is a hard country, and it takes a hard man to stay alive in it. Maybe you boys will be riding on in a day or two." He struck a match and lit his cigarette, then blew out a long plume of smoke. He went on: "Was I young and drifting around like you boys, you know what I'd do? I'd rustle me a little cash, just enough for a stake, and find an outfit I could buy. You three seem to get along real well. You might throw in together."

"I've thought about that," the Kid said. "We hit it off real good, but hell, between us, we couldn't buy the hind end of one steer."

"There's always ways of getting that stake I was talking about," Rawls said. "There's an old mining camp in the San Juans named Rolly. Used to be a boom town, but the mines played out. It's still the county seat. The county officials and the clerks and secretaries live there. That's about all, but it has got a bank. Not much in it probably, but it'd be enough."

He got up and walked off. It was dusk then, and we couldn't see very well, but we looked at each other, all three of us having the same notion. I didn't know how far the Kid and Smith had gone outside the law, although they had mentioned a bank they'd knocked over on their way south.

"We had to have eating money," the Kid had told me once in an offhand way as if the only way to get eating money was to rob a bank.

We sat there with me thinking about a cell that was waiting for me at Deer Lodge, and I came to the conclusion I had before, that, if I was going to spend the rest of my life trying to stay out of the pen, I might just as well live a little higher on the hog. I couldn't be much worse off as far as the law went than I was now.

"You boys reaching the same conclusion I am?" I asked.

"What's that?" the Kid said.

"I reckon I have," Smith said. "This Sewell *hombre* is a horse thief. I figure his cattle operation is just a blind to make him look legitimate. We said a while back that something didn't smell right here. I'd say that's what it is. I don't call myself an expert on horseflesh, but the animals Sewell brought in would be worth a pretty penny in Colorado where the law wouldn't be looking for them."

"It's my guess that's where he'll take them," I said. "You figured out why they're all wearing black duds?"

"Sure," Smith said. "It's safer to work at night when you're wearing black. Harder to see in the dark."

"I'll be damned," the Kid said. "I guess I ain't real smart. I didn't figure all that out. Makes sense, though, but why did Stub want us to move on? We've got along with him."

"I don't think he's real sure of us," I said. "We might turn his boss in."

"Or Bull Hammer might get word you're here and come sashaying out here to get you," Smith said. "Hammer would get a little nosy about the horses he'd see in the corrals. Sewell will want to slap his brand on them, so he won't be moving them out for a while."

"Bull's the kind of mean bastard who's gonna keep looking for you," the Kid said. "I'm surprised he ain't been here before this."

"I'll pull out in the morning," I said. "No use of you boys going if you like it here."

"We ain't busting up," the Kid said sharply. "Not yet anyhow. Like I told Stub, we get along real well."

34

"Like the three musketeers," Smith said. "One for all and all for one."

"Who the hell is them?" the Kid asked.

It was too dark to see for sure, but I thought Smith gave me that grave, slightly amused smile I'd seen on his face more than once. I'd read the book because it had been in my mother's library, so I knew what he was talking about, but the Kid had never read anything more complicated than what was printed on the outside of a can of tomatoes.

"Oh, it's just a story I read a long time ago," Smith said.

We told Rawls right after breakfast that we were quitting. He paid us, not seeming to be surprised. He said—"Good luck, boys."—and shook hands with all three of us. We headed for the corral, then we stopped flat in our tracks. A couple of riders were coming in from Baggs.

"Now that's one for the book," Smith said. "That's Bull Hammer and his deputy, Rip Hughes."

"We'll just lay low," the Kid said. "We got no business tangling with them this morning."

We walked on toward the corral where the crew was saddling up. Sewell and his four hardcases were getting ready to brand the horses they'd driven in the day before. Rawls had followed us to the corral, and now he yelled at Sewell: "Jerry, we've got visitors."

Sewell turned to look at the incoming riders and started toward Rawls as soon as he recognized who his visitors were, then stopped about ten feet from his foreman. We all stood motionless, waiting for Hammer and his deputy.

I was surprised when I looked at Sewell. He was bug-eyed. I had never seen a worse scared man in my life. I figured a hardcase like he was wouldn't be scared of anything or anybody, but I was wrong. He was scared of Bull Hammer, all right. It was in his eyes, in the strained expression on his face, the way the corners of his mouth were quivering.

"I thought we'd get out of here before he showed up," Sewell said to Rawls.

"What do you suppose he wants?" Rawls asked in an innocent tone.

"You know damn' well what he wants," Sewell snapped. "I didn't think we'd been spotted on the way down here, but somebody's got word to him."

Hammer and Hughes had dismounted and tied up in front of the house. Now they swaggered toward us the way bullies do. In my experience most bullies are like Sid Blackwell back home, tough on anybody they knew they could handle, and apparently they were sure they could handle anybody here.

I glanced at Sewell who was waiting exactly where he'd stopped when he'd left the corral. I turned my gaze from Sewell to Hammer and back to Sewell, and I realized Sewell was more than scared. He was petrified.

Then I did something that, looking back on it later when I had time to think, I regard as absolutely insane. It occurred to me that if I diverted Hammer's attention, I'd do Sewell a favor. Not that I gave a damn about Sewell, but the J Bar had given me a refuge for a month and a few dollars to jingle in my pockets. Besides, the trouble might include Stub Rawls, and I did owe him something.

But the hub of the matter was that I had a question that had been sticking in my craw. Ever since the Kid and Smith had hustled me out of the Baggs saloon, I'd been wondering if I could handle Bull Hammer. I decided it was time to find out.

I walked toward the law man who had reached Sewell and stopped in front of him, saying: "You're up to your old tricks, ain't you, Jerry? I want to see your bill of sale for them horses you've got in the corral?"

"Hammer," I called, "you still got the lump on your noggin I gave you in Baggs about a month ago?"

He wheeled toward me, his face turning red in an explosion of anger. He forgot all about Sewell's horses. "Well, by God," he said as if he couldn't believe it, "so you're the huckleberry who slugged me. I've been looking all over for you." He stripped off his gun belt and handed it to his deputy. "I'm gonna make you sorry you ever rode into Baggs."

I handed my gun belt to Smith, not looking at him or the Kid, but I knew what they were thinking, that they'd saved my hide once, but this time I was on my own. I took a couple of steps toward Hammer, suddenly wondering if I had been a complete idiot in challenging the man.

Hammer was bigger and stronger than I was, and he was a brutal man. It was there in his ugly, vein-splotched face. He started walking toward me, his fists cocked in front of him, a predatory animal who was sure of his prey. He'd maim me by biting an ear off or gouging my eyes out or kicking my balls to pieces.

I'd fought big men before, so I knew what to expect, and I certainly knew what I had to do—stay out of his bear-like hugs that would smash my ribs, if he got his hold on me. Too, I had to put him away quickly. If I didn't, he'd wear me down and finish me in his own way and time.

He was grinning when he reached me and threw a right at my face. His fist looked as big as a horse's hoof coming at me, but he was slow. It was not the way I expected him to fight. I ducked under his fist and caught him on the nose with a short, vicious right. His nose flattened, and blood flew like the juice of a stepped-on cherry. He bellowed in pain, the sound an angry bull might make. He was well-named.

He rushed me then, his huge hands extended to grab me around the middle. I side-stepped and caught him on the ear with a good, looping punch that spun him half around. After that it was a matter of staying out of his grip and peppering him with blows. I couldn't get in the kind of punch that would have ended it, but the longer it went, the worse off I was, and he was just gathering steam.

Suddenly he changed tactics and stopped rushing and starting punching. I kept side-stepping and moving my head so most of his blows missed, but after a few minutes of that kind of maneuvering I made a mistake, and he caught me on the side of the head, and I went down, a crazed feeling rushing through me that his punch had knocked my head off my shoulders.

I rolled over and rolled again sheerly by instinct as he tried to fall on me, but he missed, his knees hitting the dirt beside me. I couldn't think straight for a few seconds and don't remember what happened next, but I know I got astraddle of him and grabbed a handful of hair and pounded his face into the dust.

He shook me off and struggled to his feet, but I was waiting for him, and, just as he stood up, I got in the punch I'd been waiting to give him, a driving uppercut that caught him squarely on the jaw. He went down about as pretty as he had in the Baggs saloon.

I retreated toward the corral and leaned against the bars. I said to the deputy: "Get him on his horse and vamoose."

Everyone else stared at Hammer who wasn't moving, and then at me. I was still leaning against the corral bars, and my head hadn't stopped spinning. If I hadn't hit him in the right place at that particular time, he'd have finished me. I just couldn't think clearly, and there seemed to be two Hammers lying on the ground. I was finally realizing he'd hit me more than I thought he had.

The deputy brought the horses. Hammer was on his hands and knees by that time. With the deputy's help, he lifted himself into the saddle. His nose was still bleeding, one eye was closed, and he had a cut on the side of his face that was bleeding worse than his nose. They rode off, Hammer hanging onto his saddle horn.

"You done it," the Kid crowed. "You're a better man than I figured you were."

"A good job," Rawls said, "but you'd better make yourself scarce around here. Hammer will kill you, if he ever catches up with you."

Then something happened I couldn't believe. Sewell came unstuck, and he walked toward me, so angry he was trembling. "You son-of-a-bitch," he said. "You make an enemy out of Hammer, and then you come crawling out here to hide and bring him down on the rest of us. I'm going to give you the beating of your life."

On another occasion I could have finished him off in a hurry, but not this morning. My fight with Hammer had taken too much out of me. I was still shaken up, and I wasn't seeing the world the way it was. I just stood staring at Sewell, not understanding why he was threatening me.

He drew back his fist to hit me, but before he could swing, the Kid said: "Sewell, you touch him and I'll blow your head off."

Sewell turned to stare at the Kid who held his cocked gun in his hand. One look at the Kid's face must have convinced him that he meant what he said.

Sewell sucked in a long breath and bellowed: "You're fired."

"They've already quit," Rawls said quickly. "Let 'em ride off, Jerry."

Sewell dropped his fist, his four men coming out of the corral just as Smith handed me my gun. I buckled it around me as Smith said: "You boys back up and stay there. All we want is to get out of here, but, if you push us, there'll be a few dead men on the ground, Sewell being the first to drop."

They backed up, and I guess Sewell began thinking a little straighter and figuring it wasn't worth getting killed over. He said: "Drift."

I glanced at Rawls who was staring at Sewell in distaste. He nodded at me. "Jerry won't stop you."

We saddled up and were on our way south before Sewell could change his mind. We didn't talk until we were across the river. My head was hurting like hell, my shoulders and arms were just one big screaming ache, and I knew I wasn't going to stay on my horse much longer.

We forded the Little Snake and pulled up in a grove of cottonwoods, and I just sort of spilled out of my saddle. Smith said: "I'll pull your saddle off for you. You take it easy."

"Did he hit me more than once?" I asked.

"A few more times," Smith said dryly. "You took a lot of his punches on your arms and shoulders, and they shook you up. His fists are like mule kicks."

"I don't know about you, Del," the Kid said. "Either you're a brave man or a damn' fool, and I'm inclined to think you're a fool."

"Feeling the way I do right now," I said, "I can't argue with you."

I had proved I could handle Bull Hammer, but, as I lay there in the grass beside the river staring up at the blue sky, the cottonwood leaves dancing above me, I told myself I really hadn't proved anything except, as the Kid said, I was a damned fool. I'd had more luck than sense. I'd let my pride get me into something that had just about been more than I could handle. I told myself I'd never let it happen again.

# Chapter Five

We remained beside the river for several hours, the Kid getting antsier by the minute. Finally he said: "Del, if you can stick on a horse for a while, we oughta be moving."

I didn't think Bull Hammer was in any shape to come after us today, but I knew what was in the Kid's mind. He didn't want to tangle with the big man any more than I did, especially if he brought a posse. In any case, we didn't have a pound of coffee or a slab of bacon between us, so we couldn't stay here indefinitely even as pleasant as it was in the shade.

"I'll try," I said.

Smith saddled up for me, and I hoisted myself into leather, every muscle in my arms and chest and shoulders screaming in pain, but I gritted my teeth and hung on. We rode till late in the afternoon when we came to a ranch. We stayed overnight there and got two meals. They could see that I was bunged up, so I told them I'd been bucked off a horse and that satisfied them.

I felt some better the next day, but I was still bruised up and felt it. We reached the Yampa and turned downstream until we came to Craig where we bought supplies, then rode south again. We took it easy for several days, avoiding towns until we ran out of grub, but by the time we reached Montrose we figured we were far enough from Baggs that Hammer's influence wouldn't reach us.

We asked about Rolly, trying to make it sound casual, not wanting to make anyone think we really were interested in the town so they'd hook us up later on with the bank robbery. We learned enough to know that once we got past Trout Lake, we couldn't miss Rolly. I was uneasy, telling myself that once I had a hand in a bank robbery, my future was decided for me.

The more I thought about it, the less I liked the prospect of being on the run all my life, or being sent to prison, or getting shot to death by a posse. Or, for that matter, having to shoot some posse member to stay free.

I didn't mention it until we reached Trout Lake and camped beside it. We cooked our supper and sprawled in the grass at the edge of the water, the Kid saying he wished we had some fishing tackle. Any lake named Trout Lake ought to have some fish.

Then I knew I had to say what was on my mind, and I blurted: "Kid, just how deep are you in trouble with the law?"

He took the cigarette out of his mouth he'd been smoking. "What the hell difference does it make?"

I didn't want to tell him how much I'd been kicking around the notion that I'd be smarter to take off by myself and get a riding job and stay out of more trouble. It seemed to me there was a chance that in time the charges might be dropped, so if I didn't commit a crime now, I'd be in the clear.

"I was just thinking," I said. "If you and John aren't in too much trouble, maybe it would be a good idea not to do anything that would put you in deeper."

"I'm up to my neck, if that's any help," the Kid said sharply. "If you want to pull out now, say so, but I've got no choice. I can't be no worse off. I've killed three men, and I've held up or helped hold up six banks."

"Where'd all the *dinero* go?" I asked.

He laughed. "I'll tell you one thing, Del. I never have had no trouble getting rid of my *dinero*. I gambled most of it away. I guess some floozies in Helena and Butte got the rest."

"All right, we'll go ahead with this Rolly bank," I said. "You willing to give up spending your share to buy that ranch Stub was talking about?"

"You bet I am," he said quickly. "It ain't so much I'm going to change. I never will, I reckon, but on the other hand I'd like the feeling of owning something myself and working with partners I trusted. Trouble is, I don't have no idea whatever of where we'd find a little spread where we'd feel safe."

"I don't know for sure," Smith said. "I do know it will take some looking, but there's bound to be places in Nevada and Arizona where nobody would identify us. I guess it would make hermits out of us, but I could stand that. I don't know about you fellows, though."

"Oh, I can," the Kid said.

I didn't believe him, and I wasn't sure how I'd get along, but I didn't say so. Instead, I said: "One more thing. I don't figure we'll get enough out of the Rolly bank to buy this spread we're talking about."

"Then we'll hit another bank," the Kid said quickly. "You ain't thinking like an outlaw yet, Del, and it's time you started. A man like us can't go back, damn it. All we can do from here on in is to keep from being thrown into the calaboose."

"How about you, John?" I asked. "You in as deep as the Kid?"

"To all intents and purposes, I am," he said. "I helped him hold up one bank, and that's enough if I'm ever recognized. But the real point is I'm facing a first degree murder

44

charge back home. Nothing can ever change that."

"The Kid told me about it," I said. "It strikes me you'd have a good chance to be acquitted, if you tried. In most communities it would be called justifiable homicide. I guess the theory is that you defended your home, killing this man, and it's an unwritten law that you have a right to do that."

"I know," he said wearily, "and maybe I should have stayed and faced the music, but the trouble was the man I killed was the Number One gent in the community. He's got two brothers who, along with him, called the turn. No, they'd have stretched my neck." He leaned forward and added: "The Kid's right, Del. We can't look back. We go ahead. I'd like to think of myself living some place where a law man wouldn't be coming up behind me and shoving a gun in my back. I'd like to find another woman, have children, and settle down and forget the past."

I nodded, finding that understandable. I knew him and the Kid pretty well by this time. In his heart the Kid was an outlaw. He probably had been all his life. He thought like an outlaw. He had an outlaw's contempt for law men. The fact that he had killed three men did not make a feather's weight of difference to him. On the other hand, he was a good friend, and I did not doubt that, if he had had occasion to shoot Bull Hammer or Jerry Sewell in my defense, he would have done so without a moment's hesitation.

On the other hand, John Smith was not basically an outlaw, and I sensed that he regretted killing the man he had found in bed with his wife, and he regretted even more holding up the bank. He was a smart man who weighed the odds, and, having given way once in a moment of passionate hatred, he had accepted his destiny and so would probably continue being an outlaw.

Smith was a town man, but he was also a good cowboy

who held up his end of whatever job he was on. I felt akin to him more than to the Kid, yet in a showdown I thought the Kid was the one I would depend on, maybe because Smith had little confidence and would probably need to consider a situation before he committed himself.

I thought about him a moment, studying him in the firelight, then said: "John, I'm surprised you have any use for women after your experience with your wife."

He filled his pipe, glanced briefly at me, and didn't say a word until he had his pipe going, then he said: "Del, you will think I'm a complete idiot, and I wouldn't argue the question, but I still love my wife. I would take her back, if I could. I know I can't and will not be able to, but someday there might be another woman in my future if I'm lucky enough to find her."

"If I were in your boots," I said, "I don't think I would feel that way."

"I know damned well I couldn't," the Kid said. "Hell, you should have plugged her, too."

"No," Smith said. "I knew what she was when I married her. I loved her anyhow. I still do. She just can't turn a man down, and she was pretty enough to excite any man who had anything to do with her. Shannon, the man I shot, was a likable gent who could talk his way out of a grizzly's grip, and he simply took advantage of her. She couldn't help doing what she did."

"If you took her back," I said, "it would be the same thing over again."

"Of course," he said. "I'd still take her back."

"I sure don't savvy that," the Kid said.

I didn't, either. "Takes all kinds to make a horse race," I said, and let it drop there. I nodded at the Kid. "How are we going to work it tomorrow?"

"Why, we'll just ride into town like any other cowboys who are looking for work," the Kid said. "We'll put our horses in a livery stable and get a room in the hotel, if there is one. We'll look the town over, eat breakfast in the morning, then hit the bank as soon as it opens."

"How are we going to leave town?" I asked.

"Right down the cañon," he said, "if it looks the way I'm thinking it does. We'll be riding uphill if we come back this way, and I sure don't want to be slowed down. Besides, there's bound to be some timber the other way. If anything goes wrong, we'd have a better chance to hide out. I ain't never been here before, so I don't know what it's like up on the pass, but chances are it'll be above timberline and as bare as a baby's bottom."

"We'd better buy up some grub tomorrow night," I said.

"Yeah, it wouldn't hurt," the Kid agreed, "but I don't figger on nothing going wrong."

We went to sleep not long after that, at least the Kid and John did. I didn't sleep much, just in and out, and I dreamed a lot, mostly about a sheriff as big as Bull Hammer. I got to thinking about what Cæsar said when he crossed the Rubicon. My high school teacher said it had been a big decision, and Cæsar must have thought about it for days before he decided to march on Rome.

I don't know about Cæsar, but I had a hard time before dawn began to spread its opalescent light over the lake. I kept going back over the same ground, arguing it back and forth with myself, but I never reached the point where I decided to pull out. After I'd sorted it all out, it seemed to me it was the way Smith said. I couldn't go back home; I couldn't figure on being so lucky that the charges would be dropped.

We got up before the sun showed above the mountain

wall on the east. We built a fire and cooked breakfast, a sharp breeze blowing in off the lake. I had never seen peaks as high as these in the San Juans, and they amazed me just as I was amazed by how chilly the morning air was here in the middle of summer.

An hour later we rode south, following a steep trail up the mountain that bordered the lake, our long shadows following our progress. Presently we saw on our right the pillar of rock that gave Lizard Head Pass its name. Once over the top, it was downhill all the way to Rolly, much of the time in the bottom of a steep-walled cañon, the river boiling below us at the base of the cliff.

We rode into Rolly in the middle of the afternoon. As I had expected from what Stub had said, it was more ghost town than a real, living county seat. It was a long, narrow town that ran like a ribbon in the bottom of the cañon, with huge mining dumps scattered above us on the sides of the mountains. Here and there we could see the gaunt, skeletal remains of mills that had worked the ore from the mines, grim reminders of the activity that had gone on here years ago.

The town itself was made up largely of log cabins, most of them empty with windows knocked out and doors askew. The business part of town was one long block with a few stone or brick buildings, one of which was the bank. I made a mental note of its location as we rode the length of the block and went on as far as a bridge that spanned the river below Rolly. It marked the edge of town, so we turned back and left our horses in a livery stable.

Most of the buildings had their windows boarded up and the front doors padlocked, but there was some evidence that a few people lived here, probably, as Stub had said, the county officials and their office help.

The courthouse was a brick building set on a bench above the business block. It seemed too pretentious for a county the size of this one. A couple of horses wearing the Diamond M brand were racked in front of one of the saloons. Two cowboys were hunkered down on the boardwalk beside the batwings. They stared at us curiously as we pushed past them and went in, but neither said anything.

We ordered beers and stood talking to the bartender about the town and what it had been in the old days, days that really weren't that long ago, although judging from the appearance of Rolly a man would think it had been many years.

"Rolly will come back, " the barkeep said. "You boys just wait and see. Lots of silver still in the mines. Just needs a market to pay for getting it out." He took a long breath, and added: "You should have seen some of the floozies we used to have here. They were sure purty, purty to men who spent their days underground." He shook his head. "Hell, now you have to go to Durango to find a woman to sleep with, and she won't be worth a damn when you find her. Not much left hereabouts. Nothing to keep the town going except a few cattle outfits and a little dry farming."

Later we crossed the street to Grandma's Beanery and bought foot-long steaks and covered them with ketchup, swallowed three or four cups of black coffee, and went back into the street. We walked the length of the business block, noting the names of the businesses that had once occupied them and talking about how it must have been a lively camp. We wound up in the same saloon where we'd had our beer.

The Kid and Smith got into a poker game with the two cowboys who had been hunkered in front when we first were in the saloon. I didn't want any part of it. I'm a lousy gambler because it always shows in my face when I get a good hand. So I watched for a while, thinking the Kid would lose the few dollars he had left, but he fooled me. He was really a good poker player, and during the half hour I watched he pulled in ten dollars or more.

I was tired, not having slept much the night before, and told Smith and the Kid I was going to roll in. Smith nodded and said they'd be along directly. I walked the length of the business block again, wondering if I'd sleep any better than I had the night before. I suppose that if I'd robbed as many banks as the Kid had, I'd feel as casual about it as he did, but, since I wasn't in the habit of robbing banks, I found myself getting more nervous by the minute.

Finally when it was full dark, I crossed the hotel lobby and climbed the stairs to our room which was in the front of the building overlooking Main Street. I fished the key out of my pocket and was opening the door of our room when I heard a scream from the room across the hall.

It was a woman's voice. That surprised me because I hadn't seen many women around town since we'd ridden in. The second thing that surprised me was that the scream seemed to be cut off in the middle. I'd heard women scream when they're scared, and they never stop in the middle. The screams go on and on until the women run out of breath.

I stood there in the doorway for maybe five seconds, not wanting to butt in, but having a hunch I'd better find out what was going on in the room across the hall. I wheeled around and crossed the hall and tried to open the door, but it was locked. I backed up a step and kicked the door open, and then I stopped, dead still in my tracks for another second, unable to believe what I was seeing. A man was standing over the head of the bed, a pillow in his hands, and was pressing it down against the face of what looked like a girl who was kicking and threshing around and struggling to free herself. It took less than one more second for me to get it through my head that the man was murdering whoever was on the bed.

# Chapter Six

I made it to the bed in three long strides. I grabbed the man by the shoulders and yanked him around and hit him on the jaw. He had been so intent in smothering the girl that he hadn't heard me kick the door open and was completely surprised. He went back and down, the pillow falling from his hands.

I didn't take time to look at the girl. All I could think was that this fellow was a murdering bastard who didn't deserve to live. I also realized that he'd murder me, too, if he had a chance. He raised up off the floor as he dragged his gun out of his holster and lined it on me, but I didn't give him a chance to pull the trigger. I kicked him in the face, the toe of my boot catching him squarely on the chin. His head jerked back, banging against the floor. I guess he bit the end of his tongue off because blood began pouring out of his mouth.

He was out cold, but I didn't take any chances. I grabbed his gun off the floor and threw it under the bed, then I turned to the girl. Her nightgown had been torn off one shoulder, exposing a round, fully formed breast, so I knew she was not the child I had first thought, but a grown woman. The bed covers had been kicked off in the struggle and her nightgown had been pulled up to her hips.

For a moment I thought she was dead. Her face was that white and she wasn't moving. I stood staring down at her, not knowing what to do, then I saw she was breathing. I pulled the covers back up over her and waited beside the bed as she stirred and opened her eyes. She saw me leaning over her and, realizing her breast was exposed, quickly pulled the torn gown over it.

She swallowed and started to sit up, but I pressed her back against the bed. I said: "Take it easy for a while. You're safe now."

She swallowed again, fear flowing over her pale face. I suppose she was beginning to remember what had happened to her. She whispered: "Who are you?"

"My name's Del," I said. "I've got the room across the hall. I heard you scream and kicked the door open. This jasper was trying to kill you. Who is he?"

"I don't know," she said, her voice still no more than a whisper. "I never saw him before." Then she apparently began remembering some other things and sat up, this time ignoring the fact that her nightgown had slipped off her shoulder again. "Max can hire a dozen men like him. He'll keep trying. I've got to get out of here."

"You're not in condition to go anywhere," I said. "I'll get the sheriff."

She was trembling violently, so gripped by fear that she couldn't say anything for a moment; her lips worked, but she didn't make a sound. One thing was certain. She was remembering everything that was back of this attempted murder.

"No." She got the word out finally and grabbed my arm, then more words tumbled out of her so fast that it was hard to understand what she was saying. "Don't get the sheriff. He wouldn't buck Max on anything." She jerked her head at the door. "Go outside till I dress. Take that . . . that . . . animal with you."

I still thought she wasn't in condition to go anywhere, but I had never seen a human being, man or woman, as

53

thoroughly frightened as she was. I hesitated, realizing belatedly that she was young and pretty, auburn-haired and
blue-eyed, a woman who should be enjoying life instead of
being terrified as she was. I didn't have any idea who Max
was, and I didn't know anything about local politics. All I
knew was that she had a right to be scared.

Scared or not, she had to solve her own problems, I told
myself as I grabbed the would-be killer and dragged him to
the door. I'd move the man out of her room and go to bed.
I'd saved her life. She could get herself out of the hotel
without my help.

It didn't work that way. I'd just got through the door
with the unconscious man and had started to close the door
when she looked directly at me and said in a straightforward
manner: "You saved my life. Now I belong to you, and you
have to save anything that belongs to you."

I stood staring at her, thinking I had never heard a more
preposterous statement in my life, but she meant it, all
right. My first thought was to say to hell with it and tell her
I was going to bed, then I knew I couldn't do that. I had no
intention of admitting she belonged to me, but I guess I finally got it through my head that she was helpless if
someone else did try to kill her, and if this Max, whoever he
was, would hire one killer, he might very well hire a second
one.

Not knowing what she was up against, I didn't have any
idea what I'd be up against if I helped her, but I'd never
turned down a challenge like that, and I wasn't going to
start then. Still, I figured I had a right to know what I was
getting into, but, before I could ask, she said: "Shut the
door. I'll tell you about it later. It'll only take me a minute
to dress."

I shut the door and stood there waiting beside the unconscious man, thinking this was going to be interesting, more interesting than holding up a bank and maybe more dangerous. One thing was certain. It wasn't often that a pretty girl told a man that she belonged to him. I didn't know exactly what it meant, but the notion was sure intriguing.

A minute or so later she opened the door and said: "We'd better go."

Her tone was anxious, and judging from the white, taut expression on her face she was still a very frightened woman, but I didn't move. I just stood looking at her. She was wearing a tan blouse, a green riding skirt, and boots. She wasn't more than five feet tall, and I guessed she'd weigh less than one hundred pounds. I wasn't sure how old she was, but I thought around twenty.

Her hair was disheveled, her blouse was unbuttoned part way to her belt, and she gave the appearance of being about half put together, but it didn't seem to bother her. She'd just given me the fastest example of dressing I'd ever seen a woman do, but then I'd never seen a woman as terrified as this one was.

When I didn't move, she got angry, and color began returning to her cheeks. She demanded: "Are you going to stand there all night until Max sends another man to kill me?"

"Where do you want to go?" I asked.

"Anywhere," she snapped. "Just get me out of town. Some place where Max can't find me."

Still I hesitated, knowing I had to leave word for Smith and the Kid. I said—"Just a minute."—and wheeled into my room.

The girl followed, glancing nervously along the hall before she stepped through the door. I remembered there had been a school boy's tablet on top of the bureau. I ripped out a sheet, dug a stub of a pencil out of my pocket, and wrote:

> Something's come up. Get your horses and meet me at the bridge south of town. Destroy this note.
>
> Del

I left it on the bureau, figuring they'd come into the room to see what was wrong with me since I'd told them I was going to bed, then I realized that wouldn't work because they'd just think I was asleep, so I took it into their room and left it on their bed. The girl was right on my heels, not letting me get more than a step away from her.

About then I began to worry. It was fine for her to say she belonged to me with the pleasures that such a relationship promised, but I didn't want her on my back the rest of my life. Besides, the Kid and Smith would be mad as hell for having their scheme spoiled for tomorrow. But then, maybe it wouldn't spoil our plan. I'd get the girl out of town and let her go where she damned pleased.

I had reached the door when I decided there was no reason to give up the bank robbery. I started to turn to go back to get my note when she grabbed my arm. I guess she sensed what was in my mind. All I know is that she had one hell of a grip.

"You can't just walk away and let them kill me," she cried. "If you don't stay with me, they will."

She stopped talking and began to shake, he head tipped back, her eyes on me. I don't know why her strength came back to her. Perhaps it was from sheer terror, but I realized her voice was sharp and scornful, not the whisper it had been, when she asked: "Are you afraid?"

I stared down at her, suddenly angry. "Hell, no," I said.

Then I realized she had the right to feel the way she did. She knew damned well I was starting to back out again, and I guess she was thinking I was the only hope she had.

"All right, then," she said, tugging at my arm. "We'll go down the back stairs. I don't want them to see me leave. They'll hunt for me in the hotel. When they don't find me, they'll start looking somewhere else, but that will give us enough time to get out of town."

So far nobody had come up the stairs, but she kept turning her head to see if anyone was coming. We ran down the hall to a door that opened out onto a small platform. A steep staircase led to the alley below us.

I heard her sigh in relief the instant the door closed behind us. We descended the stairs, the girl hanging onto my arm as if her life depended on me, and maybe it did. By the time we reached the alley, I was beginning to get sore again, realizing she had trapped me, but the resentment soon left me. I thought: *Why, hell, this is going to be a lot of fun.* Anyhow, I couldn't blame her for wanting to live, and she was convinced she wasn't going to live very long unless she had my help.

"We'll get horses from the livery stable," she said.

As we raced through the darkness toward the stable, I began to wonder if somebody really would try to stop us. It wasn't long until I quit wondering. The back door of the stable was directly ahead of us. A lantern hanging from a nail just above the door cast a cone of murky light on the ground below it. The girl had released her grip on my arm, and in her eagerness to get her horse she had rushed ahead until she was a full step beyond me. She couldn't think of anything except getting out of town and nearly got killed because of her one-track mind.

She had barely reached the lighted area when it occurred

to me that, if the men who wanted to kill her were trying to block all possible routes of escape, they might station a man here to keep her from getting to her horse. I grabbed her by an arm and yanked her back with my left hand as I pulled my gun with my right. I sent her sprawling, and, just as she fell, a .45 roared from somewhere ahead of me in the runway, the flash of the shot momentarily lighting up the black interior of the stable.

The dry-gulcher missed, but my answering shot didn't. I guess I just had better luck than he did. At the moment I didn't realize how good my luck had been. I went flat on my belly and crawled through the door and into the nearest stall. I waited, listening, and then a man called: "You got him. Just sit pat and I'll have a look."

I didn't move, and I didn't say anything. It might be a trick. The man who had called might be the same man who had shot at me. The stand-off didn't last more than a few seconds until the girl called: "That you, Andy?"

"It's me," he answered. "You sound like Kate."

"I am Kate," she said.

"Well, if you done the shooting, you done a good job," the man said. "You got this jasper right through the brisket. He's as dead as a side of bacon on Christmas morning."

The girl ran past me toward the man, yelling: "Come on. It's safe. That's Andy Brown. He runs the stable."

I got to my feet, still hanging onto my gun. I couldn't trust anybody, I thought, not until I knew what was going on. When I walked along the runway, the man the girl called Andy had brought another lantern from the front of the stable, and I saw he was an old, bearded fellow who didn't look any part of an outlaw. If the girl thought he was all right, I figured he was.

Andy was bending over the fallen man, holding the lantern so the light fell on his face. He was a hardcase if I'd ever seen one, but after him trying to dry-gulch us I sure as hell was prejudiced.

"Saddle Blondie for me," the girl ordered Andy, then turned to me. "You get saddled up, too, Del. The shots will bring somebody here in a hurry."

"I seen that *hombre* hanging around here early in the evening," Andy said, "but I didn't think much about it till a while ago when he poked a gun in my ribs and stuck me in a stall. He said he'd beef me if I made a sound. Was he after you, Kate?"

"Sure he was," the girl said impatiently. "Now saddle up for me. We've got to get out of here."

"I'll saddle your mare for you," Andy said, "but you can stop worrying. Nobody's gonna hurt you now."

I turned from the dead man to my horse. I wasn't so sure as Andy that nobody was going to hurt the girl now. If whoever wanted to kill her would hire two men to do the job, he was capable of hiring three. By the time I had finished tightening the cinch on my horse, Andy had led the girl's mare from her stall.

"Where you going?" Andy asked as she mounted.

"Just out of town," she said. "This is the second time tonight that Max has tried to get me killed. Don't tell anybody I've left. Let 'em hunt for me."

She rode out of the stable through the back door. I mounted and followed, and, when I caught up with her, I said: "We're heading south."

"Why?" she demanded.

"I left a note," I said, and turned toward the bridge below town.

I wasn't sure she liked the direction we took, but I noticed that she followed without any argument.

# Chapter Seven

When we reached the bridge, I said: "We'll wait here."

"No, we won't," the girl cried. "We're putting all the distance we can between us and the men Max hired to kill me."

I nudged my horse closer to hers, my temper boiling up close to the exploding point. "Damn it," I shouted at her, "you'll do what I say if you want my help. Now pull off the road and get under the bridge. Nobody will see us, if they do ride by."

She obeyed, not wanting to ride by herself, I thought grimly. I was into this now, and I was damned sure I wasn't going to stay in unless I found out what was going on. There was plenty of room for our horses on the gravel between the end of the bridge and the edge of the water, so we reined up and dismounted.

As we moved away from the horses to the grass-covered bank above the river, she demanded: "What sense is there in stopping here?"

"Because I've got a couple of friends who'll meet us here," I answered irritably. "We had plans for tomorrow, and, if I hadn't got into this fracas with you, I'd be asleep in bed, and we could have gone on with our plans."

I didn't tell her what those plans were. I guess I was just sore at her for arguing with me about stopping. It wouldn't have been smart to tell her we were planning on knocking over the bank. I knew the minute I thought about it I shouldn't be sore at her; she'd been in a hell of fear and worry, and I suppose the only thought in her head was to get as far away as she could as soon as she could.

We stood facing each other, the thin moon throwing its pale light on her face, but there wasn't enough of it to make out her expression. I put my hands on her shoulders and felt her trembling. I was ashamed of myself for not being gentler with her.

"It's all right," I said. "I'm glad we aren't going ahead with the plans we had."

"I'm sorry," she said miserably. "I can't tell you how grateful I am for what you've done. The last thing I remember was that man forcing his way into my room and hitting me and knocking me back onto the bed, and then he put that pillow over my face. . . ." She stopped and began to tremble so violently that she couldn't speak.

"You're all right now," I said. "I won't leave you till you're safe."

I guess several minutes passed before she stopped shaking. I put my arms around her and held her close, and kept repeating: "You're all right now."

When she could talk, she said: "How can you thank a person who has saved your life twice in half an hour? I told you I belong to you. I'll give you anything . . . I mean, I do. . . ."

"I don't want any woman belonging to me," I said, "so quit saying that. There is one thing I do want. If I'm going to keep on helping you, I've got to know what this is all about. It must be pretty big to make a man so hell-bent on killing you as this jasper is. I don't know who he is, but. . . ."

"His name is Max Landon," she said, "and it is big. About one hundred thousand dollars. Besides the Diamond M, Daddy had a lot of cash deposited in the Rolly bank. Plenty of women have been killed for less."

That staggered me. I just couldn't believe it. I didn't think there was that much money in this end of the state with the mines being closed down the way they were. I didn't tell her I figured she was lying, but the thought did occur to me that she might not know how much the Diamond M was worth, or how much cash he had in the bank. Then I wondered what she'd say if I had told her we were planning to rob that bank. I was glad I hadn't told her.

"Tell me about it," I said.

"My name's Kate Muldoon," she said. "My father was Red Muldoon. Ever hear of him?"

"No."

"Then I guess you're a stranger here."

"I'm from Montana," I said.

"That explains it," she said. "Daddy was well-known all over the state. I guess he was a kind of a character. Anyhow, he was a man people talk about. He brought a herd of cattle into this country when it first opened up and started the Diamond M on the river about twenty miles below here. He made a fortune selling cattle to the miners.

"The strike at Rolly was made just before he got here. We had the biggest ranch in the county, and, after the mines played out, he was the only rich man hereabouts, so he ran practically everything. He went to the state legislature for two terms. He was county commissioner almost up until he died, although he was so crippled up the last year he couldn't get out of the house. He died a week ago. I don't know how much his estate is worth, but it's my guess it will turn out to be more than one hundred thousand. Now you know what it's all about."

"Then I guess you're a rich woman," I said.

"If I live to inherit it," she agreed. "I'll tell you about Max. He drifted into Daddy's life when he was fifteen. He just rode in one evening on a horse that Daddy said wasn't worth the price of a bullet to put him out of his misery. The boy wanted to work, and, although Daddy was always tough on cowboys riding the grub line, he felt sorry for this kid. His name was Max Landon."

"That's the Max you've been talking about," I said, beginning to see the shape of what was going on.

"That's right," she said. "Mama was alive then, and the kid was so dirty she wouldn't let him in the house. Mama and Daddy fought a lot, and I guess that the way Mama treated Max made Daddy decide to let him stay. Once he got cleaned up and Daddy found some decent clothes for him, and he got food in his belly, he turned out to be the hardest worker I ever saw. That was something Daddy always admired.

"Daddy practically raised Max. Mama died soon after that. Daddy hired one housekeeper after another. Max always lived in the house after Mama died. I guess everybody knew that Daddy was fixing to have Max ramrod the outfit as soon as he was old enough. He had worked on a ranch, and he seemed to just naturally have a lot of cow savvy.

"When he was twenty, our foreman got bunged up in a stampede and had to quit. From then on, Max has been foreman and as near a son as Daddy ever had. I was supposed to be a boy, you know, and, after Mama died, Daddy never knew what to do with me. The housekeepers raised me more than he did.

"Finally Daddy sent me away to school. I guess he figured the schools could make me a lady when he couldn't. I went to Denver first, then back East. I was still there when I got a wire from Judge Bailey that Daddy had died. I got here as soon as I could, but they'd had the funeral before I got home."

"And now Max wants the Diamond M?" I said.

"It's as simple as that," she agreed.

"If you're the only child . . . ?" I began.

"I don't know what's in the will," she interrupted, "and Judge Bailey won't tell me. He did say it was a bad will, and he had tried to get Daddy to change it, but he said you know how stubborn your daddy was. He'd make a mule look like a rabbit."

She paused, and I felt her begin to tremble again, but she was able to go on a moment later. "Oh, Daddy loved me, all right. He used to take me hunting and fishing and tried to treat me like a boy, but it didn't work, so he really gave Max the love I would have had if I'd been a boy. I don't think Max is equal to me in the will. Daddy was always one to respect blood relationship. He wanted me to marry Max. That way he would keep on running the ranch. Actually he'd own it, I guess, with the law being what it is about women. Daddy wanted the ranch run right, too. He was very proud of it, and he never thought a woman could do anything."

She walked away from me, then whirled and walked back as if suddenly remembering a killer might be sneaking up on us. She said: "I can't stand Max. I never could. He's big and brutal and sneaky. I always thought he was robbing Daddy, but I never had any proof. Daddy trusted him and thought he could do no wrong. Max has been after me to marry him ever since I was fifteen, but I told Daddy I'd kill myself if he forced me to marry Max, so he didn't press me, but he let me know what he wanted."

We heard horses coming from town, and Kate ran back under the bridge. "It's them," she cried. "Come on. Don't let them see you."

"It's my friends," I said. "Max's men wouldn't have any way of knowing where you went."

She didn't like what I said, but she didn't argue this time. A moment later the riders drew up just before they reached the approach to the bridge, and the Kid called: "Del?"

"Here," I said.

They reined down the slope from the road and pulled up in front of us, the Kid leaning forward in the saddle to see me. He said angrily: "Would you mind telling me what in hell you're up to, bringing us out here . . . ?"

"I know," I said, "but just hold your horses. Come here, Kate." She stepped out from under the bridge, reluctantly, as if she didn't trust even these men who were my friends. "Kate, I want you to meet John Smith. The gabby galoot is known as the Kid. I don't know if he has any other name or not."

"I'm pleased to meet you," she said in a low voice that was little more than a whisper.

In the darkness I caught the movement of John Smith's arm as he tipped his hat. "It's an unexpected pleasure to meet you, Miss . . . ?"

"Kate Muldoon," she said.

"The beauty of the Irish language is in your voice, Miss Muldoon," he said. "I'm sure the beauty is in your face, too, if I could see you."

"You'll get a chance," I said. "We're running herd on Kate. Two men tried to kill her tonight."

"The hell," the Kid said, suddenly interested. "I suppose you saved her life."

"That he did," Kate said. "A man was smothering me with a pillow, and he smashed the door open and beat the man and threw him out of my room. He got me out of the hotel, then, when we got to the livery stable, a man tried to shoot us."

65

"Only he killed the man," the Kid said in awe. "Well, by God, Del, I didn't think you had it in you."

"Oh, but he has," Kate said quickly. "He was grand. I wish you could have seen him."

"So do I," the Kid said. "It must have been a rip-snorting show."

"A knight of old," Smith said wryly. "Are you Sir Bors, Del? Or possibly Lancelot?"

"Who the hell are them *hombres?*" the Kid demanded.

"Two heroes out of the past," Smith said. "I'm sure you never heard of them." "You know damned well I haven't," the Kid snapped. "You're always talking big about *hombres* like them. Why don't you talk about somebody I have heard of . . . like Butch Cassidy?"

I almost laughed out loud. This had been going on between them ever since I'd met them. Smith could have been a high school English teacher. He certainly knew a lot about both American and English literature. The Kid, who hadn't finished the eighth grade, always ended up pretty, and sometimes downright, sore.

Before it went that far, I said: "We've got to get Kate to some place where she'll be safe."

"Damn it," the Kid snapped. "I don't see that it's our business to run herd on a gal we've never seen before. She said you'd saved her life twice. Ain't that enough? Turn her loose to go wherever she wants to. We've got a. . . ."

"Maybe I've got something to say about this," Kate interrupted. "You're right. Turn me loose. Del has done enough. It's just that I belong to. . . ."

"All right," I broke in, having heard enough of that to last me the rest of my life. "Where can we take you?"

"There's only one place I can think of," Kate said, "and I don't know how safe it is. When I was small, Daddy used to take me there to fish. It's on the North Fork about eight or nine miles from here. When I got older, I rode up there by myself and stayed for weeks. A woman everybody calls Aunt Becky runs a sort of country hotel for people who want to fish or hunt. Or just get out of the heat in the lower altitude around Cortez and Durango."

"How do we get there?" I asked.

"Down this road about five miles," she said, "then turn up the North Fork. Her place is in a valley about three miles from the road. Aunt Becky will hide me. She knows Max, and she doesn't like him any more than I do."

"I don't know what kind of hold this woman has on you, Del," the Kid said angrily, "but she's sure leading you around by the nose. I've never seen a woman who could make me give up a scheme I'd decided on just to go chasing after her."

"Kid," Smith said, his tone carrying an edge I had never heard from him before, "your attitude is deplorable. Del and I will take this lady to her Aunt Becky. If you don't want to ride along, then ride wherever you damn' please."

"I'm going to need all three of you," Kate said. "If you will act as my bodyguards until this danger is over, I'll pay each of you one hundred dollars. It will be dangerous work."

"Just one hundred dollars?" the Kid asked. "One hundred dollars a month?"

"Per day," Kate said.

"Well, now," the Kid said, the anger going out of his voice, "you are a woman I'd chase after to hell-and-gone."

"Then let's start," Kate said uneasily. "They'll be coming after me any second."

Her fears were exaggerated, I thought, but then she knew the situation better than I did. We mounted and rode across the bridge and headed south. I thought about Kate's one-hundred-dollar-a-day offer and mentally multiplied that by thirty if this stretched out for a month.

I told myself I hoped that Kate knew what she was doing. If Red Muldoon's will didn't leave his fortune to her, or if she didn't get her hands on the money for a while, she was going to have one hell of a time paying her bill.

# Chapter Eight

We rode for what must have been two hours, staying east of the river. As near as I could tell in the thin light, we were in a valley a mile or so wide, dark ridges rising on both sides of us. I was in front with Kate, Smith and the Kid twenty feet behind us. None of us said a word until we crossed the river and Kate said: "Here's where we go up the North Fork."

We turned west and rode for another hour, climbing rapidly the first half hour, the small stream pounding below us in its rocky gorge. This side cañon we were now following was very narrow, the road itself no more than a goat trail hanging on one side of the cliff. I suppose a wagon could have used the road, but it would have required careful driving.

"One man could hold off an army in this part of the cañon," Kate said.

So she was still thinking about Max's sending some killers after her. Apparently she expected an army of them, but I couldn't see him doing that no matter how much money was involved. Max might guess she'd seek refuge here, if she had come as much as she said when she was a girl, but I doubted that he'd send more than one man. A large number would create suspicions, and I couldn't believe he was so much above the law that he wanted to spit in its face.

I didn't argue with her. Instead, I said—"There's three of us."—and let it go at that, but I did wonder how she expected us to know when his killers were coming.

After a time we rode out of the narrow cañon and into a valley. Here the road leveled off. Presently I could make out the dark but indistinct shapes of buildings ahead of us. Kate sighed and said: "We're here."

From the tone of her voice, I judged she had been afraid we'd never make it. A moment later we reined up in front of what appeared to be the house. Kate said: "Stay here. I'll get Aunt Becky up."

I stepped down, thinking I'd better go with her, and it was a good thing I did because, when she dismounted, she staggered and would have fallen if I hadn't put an arm around her and steadied her. For a moment she stood motionless, her tiny body pressed against mine.

"I'm so ashamed," she said. "I don't usually act this way. I guess I'm tired."

"You've got a right to be," I said.

She took a long breath, then she said: "I'm all right now." She walked toward the house, reached a fence, and opened a gate, saying: "She always keeps her gate closed to keep cows out of her garden."

I held one of her arms as we walked up the path to the front door. We climbed three steps to the porch and crossed it to the front door. We didn't hear anything inside the house or see a light, and Kate's knocking on the front door did not produce any sign of life, so I took a turn at pounding.

From deep inside the house a woman yelled: "I'm coming, damn it. Don't knock the place down."

Presently a light appeared in the front room and a moment later the door opened, and a woman holding a lamp in one hand shouted angrily: "What's so important that you have to . . . ?"

"Aunt Becky, it's me," Kate cried.

The woman was old, seventy or more, her hair white, her face rutted by deep lines. For just a moment she stood staring at the girl as if too amazed to believe what she was seeing, then she blurted: "Kate Muldoon, what are you doing here? I thought you were in New York. Here, let me put the lamp down." She set the lamp on a stand in the middle of the room, turned, and held out her arms. "Come here, honey. Let me hug you. I've got to find out if you're real."

Kate fled into the old woman's arms and began to cry.

The woman held her, patting her and saying over and over: "You're all right, lambie pie. You're all right." After Kate quieted down, the woman tipped her head back to stare at me. She asked truculently: "Who the hell are you?"

She was a tough old bird, I thought, but it would take that kind of woman to live in a place like this by herself. Before I could answer, Kate said: "This is Del. He saved my life twice tonight. Max tried to have me killed."

"Well," the woman sniffed. "I guess you're good for something. But Max sure as hell ain't. He's a greedy bastard, so I ain't surprised." She paused, her gaze raking me from my sweat-stained Stetson to my scuffed boots, then she asked: "Del who?"

"Just Del," I said, "or Del Del if you want a last name."

She scowled. "You sound like all the other hardcases who want to hole up here. Might as well call yourself John Smith."

"He's outside," I said.

"*Hmmph,*" she said as if she didn't believe me. "It'll cost you to use my place for a hide-out."

I knew I wasn't going to like Aunt Becky, and now I had a notion about the kind of an outfit she was running. It wasn't just a resort for hunters and fishermen, as Kate had indicated. She had a hide-out for outlaws, and she'd figured me right. Not that I had any intention of hiding out here, but she'd pegged me for what I was.

"I owe him my life, Aunt Becky," Kate said. "I want him to stay here. He has two friends outside. I've hired them as bodyguards. Max will send someone up here as soon as he hears what happened in Rolly. I'll pay for their keep while they're here."

"Two friends," the old woman said. "All cut from the same bolt of cloth he is, I guess. All right, you'll find a corral out past the barn. Use the cabin next to the house. I'll call you for breakfast, and get here on time if you want to eat."

She practically shoved me out of the door and slammed it in my face. As I walked back to where Smith and the Kid sat their saddles, I told myself that Aunt Becky might be able to look out for Kate, but beyond that I couldn't see that she had a single redeeming quality.

"There's a corral out here somewhere," I said, "and we get the cabin next to the house."

We stripped gear from our horses and turned them into the corral, then moved across the yard to the cabin that was no more than a vague shape in the darkness. I shoved the door open, struck a match, and saw that there was a lamp on a table next to the far wall. I lit it and blew out the match, then slipped the chimney into place.

The cabin had four bunks, a couple of straight-backed chairs, and a table that held a wash bowl and a white pitcher filled with water. The room was clean and smelled as if it had been aired out recently. I threw back the blankets on one bunk and saw that they were clean. I didn't think there would be bed bugs around. I didn't figure any of them were tough enough to buck Aunt Becky.

"Looks all right," I said.

Smith nodded approvingly. "Better than I had expected. What was the woman like?"

"She's an Amazon," I said. "If Max shows up here, she'll blow his head off."

The Kid was sitting on one of the bunks, tugging at a boot. "What's an Amazon?" he asked.

"A female warrior," I said.

Smith chuckled. "I was going to tell him it was a river."

"You're going to overdo that one of these days," I warned.

"I wouldn't be lying," he said defensively.

The Kid had his boots off and lay down. He said: "I'm all in, and I'm gonna sleep till noon. And Del's right. One of these days I'm gonna get damned sore, John." He turned over and gave us his back.

Smith looked at me and shrugged. He said: "My sense of humor is a little warped, I guess. I'll have to watch it."

I thought the Kid might bow to age and take one of the upper bunks, but he didn't, so I told Smith I'd take the upper and he could have the other lower one. He nodded, and, as soon as I had my boots off, he said: "Climb in and I'll blow out the lamp."

I did. A minute or two later I heard both men snoring, but, in spite of the fact that it had to be well after midnight, I didn't go to sleep for a while. I thought about Kate and what we'd have to do to earn our salaries as bodyguards. She'd probably stay here and Aunt Becky would protect her, but it was no long-term solution to her problem. She'd probably want us to stay, and that wasn't going to work if it meant a long period of time.

I figured the Kid wasn't going to sit around here doing nothing even for one hundred dollars a day. He was too antsy to stay anywhere very long, and I didn't figure I could sit here and wait for Max's plug uglies to show up. That wasn't my way. I wanted to see the Diamond M, maybe have a talk with Max, or at least size him up. I'd go into Rolly, too. I wanted to ask what Kate was up against. I couldn't believe the sheriff was as bad as she said.

The last thought that flashed through my mind was that I was relieved we weren't holding up the bank tomorrow. I just wasn't an outlaw at heart, or, as the Kid said, I didn't think like an outlaw, but before this business was over I might be an outlaw facing more than a fake rape charge.

The clanging of the triangle woke me the following morning. I sat up and rubbed my eyes that didn't want to come open. Smith was up, had his boots on, and was washing his face. I swung down, and, by the time I'd sloshed some water over my face, I finally decided I was awake.

The Kid was still sound asleep. I shook him and said: "Time to rise and shine."

"Ain't noon yet," he mumbled.

"Suit yourself," I said, "but Aunt Becky won't keep your breakfast for you, and you're always hungry by ten o'clock in the morning even when you have breakfast."

Smith and I left the cabin. When I was outside, I looked around. I found that everything was about the way I had imagined. The valley was less than a mile wide; the steep ridges on both sides were covered with pines, and willows and an occasional cottonwood grew along the creek. The house was two-story and constructed of logs, as were the three cabins, barn, and other outbuildings.

As we walked toward the house, Smith said: "This is a pleasant place to live, but damned lonely. I don't see how this Aunt Becky can stand it."

"From what I saw of her last night," I said, "she'd have

to live in a place like this because nobody could stand being her neighbor."

The house was surrounded by a stout pole fence, and, as we went through the gate, I saw a huge garden along one side of the house. The air was chilly, and I noticed that the garden was a long way from producing anything. At this altitude winters were long, summers were short, and only hardy vegetables would grow here, but by fall her turnips, cabbage, carrots, rutabagas, and the like would be mature.

The instant we went into the house through the front door, the smell of frying bacon and coffee hit me, and I realized how hungry I was. We crossed the front room which was sparsely furnished with a leather couch, three rocking chairs, and an oak stand that held a neat pile of magazines.

A huge stone fireplace made up a good part of one wall. Everything was clean and in order, and I felt a sense of admiration for the old woman who could live here by herself, do all the work that was required outside, and still keep a house as spruced up as she did. I had a hunch that the sky would fall on the man who muddied up her floor.

When we entered the kitchen, Aunt Becky was standing at the stove frying bacon. She said without turning: "Sit down. I'll have your breakfast on the table directly."

We took chairs at the long table that would have seated eight or ten people. In a matter of seconds she brought a platter of fried eggs and bacon, then poured our coffee. She stood staring at me for a moment before she said: "So, Del, Kate has been telling me about you. I guess that, if you saved her life, you're good for something, though you ain't much for looks."

"I reckon not." I nodded at Smith. "This is the John Smith I was telling you about, Missus . . . ?" I hesitated, then asked: "Or do we call you Aunt Becky?"

"Nobody calls me Aunt Becky except Kate Muldoon," she snapped. "I'm Missus Horton." She studied Smith the way she had me, then she said: "Well, I've seen a lot of John Smiths in the years I've lived here, but you don't look like the others."

"That is no doubt the gospel truth," Smith said. "I am not like the others."

"*Hmmph*," Mrs. Horton said, and stalked back to the stove with the coffee pot. "I thought there was three of you."

"The other one will be along," I said.

"He'd better hurry," she said as she took a pan of biscuits out of the oven.

Now that I had a chance to look at her in daylight I saw that she was just as old and wrinkled and tough as I had thought she was. She was tall and angular with none of the curves associated with women. Her nose was sharp, her chin a jutting rock of granite, and still I had sensed the previous night that she had a genuine love for Kate.

The Kid came in, rubbing his eyes as if he was still half asleep. He sat down beside Smith and reached for the platter of food. Mrs. Horton took a chair across from me and ate with us, her appetite as great as ours. I hadn't had a breakfast like this since I'd left Montana. The cream was yellow and thick, the biscuits tender and flaky, and the jelly just right for the biscuits. The coffee was hot and black and strong enough to float a spoon, just the way I liked it. I had earlier decided she had no redeeming qualities except her feeling for Kate. Now I had to admit she possessed one more. She was a hell of a good cook.

We didn't talk until we were on our third cup of coffee, then I asked: "Where's Kate?"

"Asleep," Mrs. Horton said.

"I want to see her," I said.

"I ain't fixing to wake her just so you can see her," Mrs. Horton snapped. "The poor lamb was so tired last night she almost fell asleep before she got her story told. She had a turrible experience. I ain't surprised that low-down cur of a Max Landon tried to have her murdered. There's a lot of money at stake. He's the kind who would want it all." She paused, picked up her coffee cup, and took a drink, then stared at me over the rim. "She can stay here as long as she likes. What do you want to see her about?"

"I don't figure on sitting here the rest of my life," I said. "She hired us as bodyguards. I want to know what she aims for us to do."

Mrs. Horton nodded. "Last night I told you it would cost you to live here, but, after Kate told me what you done for her, I've changed my mind. You can work it out for me. Del, you'll cut wood. Smith, you will hoe and weed the garden." She pointed a finger at the Kid. "And you will clean out the barn and water and feed the cow and the horse."

The Kid straightened and stared at her as if he had never heard anything as preposterous in his life. "The hell I will. I'll pay my share of. . . ."

"You'll do what I tell you," Mrs. Horton said, "or you'll get the hell out of here. It won't hurt your lily-white hands to hold a fork handle."

The Kid opened his mouth, looked at me, then shrugged. "Maybe it won't."

"All right, get to work," Mrs. Horton said. "You've been fed. I'll send Kate out to the woodpile if she wakes up before you're done."

We rose and walked out of the house through the back door, the Kid muttering: "Bank robbers, hell, we're nothing but a bunch of farmhands."

# Chapter Nine

I found a pile of cord wood back of the house, some cut from green timber, some from dead trees. Mrs. Horton must have a man around somewhere who cut her wood and maybe helped with the work around the place, I thought. I picked up the bucksaw and started. By noon I had sawed up enough wood into sixteen-inch lengths to last her a week or more. There wasn't much that was cut when I started, so I had the notion that she did her own sawing.

Mrs. Horton banged the triangle at noon, one of the most welcome sounds I ever heard. Smith caught up with me before I reached the back door, holding his back and grimacing. "I always liked working in my garden when I was home," he said, "but my garden was a postage stamp compared to this one. I don't think she's been in her garden for two weeks. Part of the time I had trouble finding the carrots among the weeds."

I looked at the blisters on my hands. "I'm about ready to tell her we'll pay for our board and room," I said. "Another half day like this and I couldn't hold a gun."

"Me, too," he agreed.

By the time we had finished washing up, the Kid came around the corner of the house, rubbing his eyes. I looked at him, and winked at Smith. I didn't have much idea whether the Kid had done a lick of work or not, but he'd been asleep, and I had a hunch his work hadn't detracted much from his sleeping.

Mrs. Horton had dinner on the table when we entered

the kitchen. She motioned toward the pump and wash basin. "Wash up and then sit down."

Before I reached my chair, Kate came into the kitchen from the living room. She was wearing the same clothes she had the day before, not having the opportunity to bring any from home, I thought, although I found out later she had left some here from the last time she had been fishing with her father. Today Kate looked like a different woman. Her hair was brushed and pinned up in a bun on the back of her head; she was rested, and, although I had not seen her before in daylight, I'd had the impression she was a very pretty girl. Now I saw that my impression had been right. Her eyes were a beautiful blue with an imp dancing in each one of them, and there was a mass of freckles on the tip of her snub nose. I also saw that, as small as she was, she was no child, but a fully developed young woman.

She crossed the kitchen to me, smiling, and, when she reached me, she hugged and kissed me, and said: "I'm alive. I'm breathing, and I'm thankful to you."

I thought she was going to start again on the business of belonging to me, but she didn't. She turned toward the other two, looking from John Smith to the Kid and back to Smith. She said: "You must be John Smith."

"That I am," he said, "and may I say you are, indeed, as pretty in looks as your voice was beautiful last night."

"Flattery," she said, smiling, "is a passport to friendship." She held her hand out, and Smith took it, then she turned to the Kid, saying: "And you are the Kid."

His face was as red as a bright sunset. I had never seen him embarrassed before, but he was now. It was my guess that he had never been around a woman like Kate Muldoon, and he didn't know how to respond. He nodded, swallowed, and finally said: "Yes, ma'am."

"I thank both of you for coming along," she said. "I hope Aunt Becky has made you welcome. I apologize for not getting up in time to have breakfast with you, but I couldn't seem to make my body get out of bed." She turned to me. "I just lay there enjoying being able to breathe. That doesn't sound like much until you find you can't breathe, and then it becomes more important than anything else in the world."

"I know how it is," Smith said. "I've had my wind knocked out of me a couple of times."

"But that was different, Mister Smith," she said. "You know that sooner or later your breath will come back, but, when a man is jamming a pillow over your face and your breathing has stopped and you know you are not strong enough to fight him off, you have every right to think you will never take another breath. That was the last thought I had before everything went black." She nodded at me. "That's why I belong. . . ."

"I'm hungry," I broke in, determined to stop her saying that even if I had to gag her. "Your Aunt Becky has been working us like dogs all morning."

"*Hmmph*," Mrs. Horton said. "John Smith looks like a bank clerk, the Kid looks like an outlaw who's moving from one bank-robbing job to another, and you look like a cowboy who's riding the grub line and don't know nothing but cowboying Hard work ain't gonna hurt none of you. Now sit down and eat."

Kate shook her head as she took a chair at the table. "Aunt Becky, it's good to be honest and forthright, but don't you think you overdo it?"

"I say what I think," she said as she took the chair at the head of the table. "If anybody don't like it, they know where their horses are."

We started to eat, too hungry to argue with the old woman, but my feeling of not liking her grew with leaps and bounds. Still, she was a good cook, and I could forgive a lot of shortcomings in exchange for the food she put on the table: steak, gravy, beans, biscuits, honey, coffee, and custard pie.

Kate cut off a bite of steak, chewed, and looked at me. She said: "You see why Daddy and I always liked to come here to fish?"

I swallowed, cut off another bite of meat, and nodded. I saw no reason to stop eating long enough to carry on a conversation with Kate.

When we finished after two helpings of everything on the table, Mrs. Horton said: "You boys have worked hard this morning. Go fishing this afternoon if you want to. The creek's too high to catch anything, but you might enjoy it. You'll find poles in the barn."

Kate rose. "I want to talk to Del." She looked at Smith, then at the Kid. "Last night you agreed to work for me. Now that you've had time to think about it, does our deal still go?"

"Sure," Smith said.

The Kid had recovered his composure, and his natural cynicism had returned. "You'll excuse my asking, ma'am, but I always look at my hole card. You're gonna owe us a lot of money. You sure you can pay?"

Mrs. Horton burst out laughing. "Young man, I guess you don't know, but Kate is the daughter of Red Muldoon, and Red could buy and sell everybody else in the county. He died a few days ago. Kate's the only heir."

The Kid stared at Kate in awe. "Well, I'll be damned. I never seen a rich woman before in my life."

"In all honesty," Kate said, "I'm not rich now. I will be in a few days, but I haven't seen the will. This man, Max Landon, thinks that if I'm killed, the estate will go to him, and I suppose it will. That's why I need you men. You've got to keep me from being murdered, or you won't get paid. I know Max well enough to be sure your job is a dangerous one."

"Ma'am," Smith said, "danger is our meat. The Kid here goes out of his way to spit into the face of rattlesnakes. Now I don't know about Del. He may run before the first cap is cracked."

"John Smith," Kate cried, "I'm ashamed of you. Del is the bravest man I ever met, and I will not stand still and let you. . . ." She stopped and glared at Smith, then smiled. "You're having fun with me. I guess I'm a little touchy after what happened last night. You wouldn't be sitting here eating with me if Del had not gone past my room when he did."

I got up from the table, not liking Smith's sense of humor. I said: "Let's take a walk, Kate. We can't have a sensible talk around here."

She wrinkled her nose at Smith. "You can stay here and visit with Aunt Becky. Del's right. The talk we've been having is not sensible."

*"Hmmph,"* Mrs. Horton said. "I've got too much work to do to sit and visit with the likes of him. With you gone, there'll be less chance than ever for sensible talk."

Kate took my arm, and we left the house. Smith was grinning as if he was enjoying himself. I said: "Your Aunt Becky is a tough old bird."

Kate nodded. "She's had to be. She's been by herself most of the time. She came here about twenty years ago with her husband and built the place, then he died, and she's made out by herself except for old man Chalk who lives up the creek a mile or two. He helps her with the hard work, cuts her wood, and puts up her hay and the like. He brings her supplies from Rolly so she doesn't have to leave the valley. I don't suppose she's been away from home in the last five years."

"She must get some hardcases in here," I said.

Kate glanced at me quickly, then looked away. "You've figured it out."

"It wasn't hard," I said.

"What I told you about people coming here to hunt and fish is true," Kate said, "but it's the longriders who pay her big money to stay. She knows how to handle them. Daddy used to try to get her to come and work for him on the Diamond M. He told her that someday one of her boarders would kill her, but she says that won't happen. Too many men owe their life to her. If anyone ever hurt her, he wouldn't live a week."

I wasn't so sure of that, but I didn't argue the point. We reached the creek and sat down on a log, the water lapping at our feet. There was a break in the willows in front of us, and we sat there for a time in silence, looking at the swift stream that was roily now with the spring run-off bringing it out of its banks.

Kate reached for my hand and took it, apparently finding some comfort, I guess, in my presence. I had never been around a woman who was as straightforward and honest as Kate. She seemed to be lacking in the subterfuges and deceptions that I had found in the girls I had gone with. I liked her very much, but, on the other hand, I was a little uneasy with her, maybe because of the way she kept talking about belonging to me. I just didn't know what to make of it.

"Aunt Becky said you wanted to talk to me," Kate said

after a long silence. "I didn't come down to breakfast because I just couldn't get myself out of bed. I'm still scared, Del. I had a crazy feeling this morning, lying there in bed warm and safe, but I kept watching the door, wondering if any minute somebody was going to come in and kill me."

"You're safe here," I said. "At least so long as Smith, the Kid, and I are here. That was what I wanted to talk to you about. You can't stay here forever. Neither can we."

"No," she agreed, "but please stay for a while. I don't feel like going anywhere right now. I want all three of you to stay here and see that I'm safe."

"All right," I said. "For a while. But what are we to do after that? You're not going to get Max off your back or inherit the Diamond M by hiding here."

"I know," she said, and shivered as she pressed against me.

"Do you have any friends in Rolly?" I asked.

"Oh, yes," she said, "but the men are old and couldn't stand up to Max. Men like Judge Bailey. He's honest and wants to do right, but the law in this county is more imagination than reality. It's the same with the banker, Adam Jessup. Same with Doc Carter. Windy Holt is the sheriff. He's a young man and honest enough, but I wouldn't trust him with my life."

"Sooner or later you've got to face a hell of a tough situation," I said. "As long as you're here and Landon has possession on the Diamond M, you're out of it."

"Tell me what to do," she said.

"I've been thinking on it," I said. "Do you have any friends on the Diamond M? Any of the riders who worked for your dad and would fight for you?"

"I haven't been out there this summer," she said, "but the judge told me the only one that was left was the cook,

Bill Rogers. He was with Daddy when they brought the first herd over the San Juans from the San Luis Valley. The judge told me that Max had fired the old crew and hired men who would be loyal to him."

"All right," I said. "I'll tell you what I want to do. I'll ride into Rolly and have a talk with the judge and the rest of your friends. I just want to size things up. Then I'll go out to the Diamond M, and maybe I'll run into Max. I want to see for myself just what kind of huckleberry he is. Sometimes a funeral or two is the only way to settle this kind of business when the law won't or can't do anything."

"I'm afraid the funeral may be yours or Smith's or the Kid's," she said morosely. "I don't want that to happen."

"Neither do I," I said, "but it's the risk we have to take." I thought about it a moment, then I added: "It seems to me that the first thing to do is to find out just what's in your daddy's will."

"We were to have read that today," she said. "I guess that was why Max wanted me killed last night."

"Then we'll have to set another date," I said.

"Suppose we read the will," she said, "and find the ranch is mine legally, but Max won't move out. What do we do then?"

"We'll see what your sheriff will do," I said. "Maybe we can put a little sand in his craw."

"Then that's when we'll have the funerals," she said. "I know Max well enough to be sure he'll never give up."

"From what you've said about him, I would expect that," I said.

Suddenly she began to tremble just as she had the night before. She whispered: "Hold me, Del, I know I'm safe when I'm in your arms."

I put an arm around her, and presently she stopped

trembling. I looked down at her and decided that holding her was a very pleasant duty, something a man seldom got paid for doing, but I also knew it was a duty that was not likely to last beyond the instant when Max Landon was killed, and that, I told myself, was a fact I had better not forget.

## Chapter Ten

For a week we did nothing but eat and sleep and enjoy ourselves at Mrs. Horton's place. I kept enough wood saved up so we didn't use what I had cut that first morning I was here. Smith spent part of each morning in the garden. Once he had caught up with the weeds, his job was easy. The Kid was edgy as I knew he would be. He went through the motions of cleaning out the barn and corrals. He did take good care of the stock because he liked animals, but most of the time he was as restless as an ant in an ant hill.

On the fifth day the Kid announced he was going hunting. He saddled up and, taking his Winchester, rode up the valley. When he returned in the afternoon, he brought in a young buck, so we had fresh meat for a change. Kate didn't like the Kid's riding off that way, but she sensed the Kid was as mercurial as the weather, so she kept her mouth shut.

It seemed to me that the Kid should have been satisfied with the money he'd earned that week, but being satisfied with anything was not in the Kid's make-up. The next day he told us he was tired of sitting around on his ass just waiting for the killer to show up. I told him we'd made a deal, and it was up to us to stick to it. He looked at me sourly and walked off.

"You might as well let him alone," Smith said. "You 'n' me can look after Kate."

I knew that, but it graveled me that the Kid had made a bargain and now he wasn't aiming to keep his word. I had the Kid pretty well sized up by this time, and I knew Smith was right. He'd told me once that the Kid was born to hang or be shot, and the longer I was around the Kid, the more I was convinced that Smith was right about that, too.

As for me, I enjoyed that week more than any other week in my life. I spent most of my time with Kate. She'd help with the housework in the morning, then we'd have the afternoon together, and usually the evening, too, after the dishes were washed and dried and put away. I realized more and more what a fine young woman she was. The fear that had plagued her the first day or two after we met had pretty well faded.

I had the uneasy feeling she had fallen in love with me. I think I hoped it was true, but then again I didn't. I'd thought about getting married for several years, and my mother had been nagging me about it, but I just hadn't been ready, mostly, I think, because I had been stuck in a little area in northern Montana all my life, and I had kept telling myself there was a big world out there for me to see. I guess I just hadn't been anxious enough to explore it to start out. I had now, and I wasn't very happy with the world in which I found myself.

I often wished I could go back and live through those hours when I'd danced with Ruby Prentiss and had taken her home. Of course, that was fantasy thinking, and all I could do now was to make the most of what I had, and that included spending time with Kate Muldoon. I didn't tell her my real reason for leaving Montana, or what we had come to Rolly to do. I wasn't real proud of either.

We rode a lot, usually up the valley past old man Chalk's place. We usually stopped to visit with him. He was as old or older than Mrs. Horton, a gray, bearded, stoop-shouldered man, but he seemed healthy and strong, and apparently was able to do the hard work that had to be done in an isolated place like this, both for his and Mrs. Horton's existence.

"He's asked Aunt Becky to marry him a dozen times," Kate told me, "but she's too independent. She's always been kind to me, but I know she's hard to get along with. She knows it, too, so she tells him they're happier this way than if they were married. I think she's right, too."

I didn't try to fish, the water being too high, and I didn't go hunting. I knew this would be a brief and peaceful interlude in my life, and I found it very welcome after what had happened to me from the time I had taken Ruby Prentiss home.

Kate told me about her childhood, the mother she'd loved, the housekeepers who had been kind to her, the school in New York she had hated because it had tried to curb her spirit and failed. I had the feeling that nothing could do that except the fear of being murdered by Max Landon, a possibility that was never out of her mind. I sensed there was more to that than she told me, but I didn't press her.

"I feel safe when I'm with you," she said one time while we were riding. "I wake up at night so scared I can't sleep, and I wish you were in bed with me. I lie there and hear noises and think someone is coming after me. I've never really been afraid of anything before in my life. What am I going to do, Del?"

"I don't think Missus Horton would stand for me being in bed with you," I said.

She laughed. "No, I don't think she would. You know, Del, I've never met a man like you. I guess that's why I like you so much. When I was home, Daddy kept a tight rein on me, so boys were afraid to even talk to me. In school I never had a chance to meet boys." She reached out and took my hand. "Now I find a man who saves my life twice, and I know that pretty soon he'll be riding away and I'll never see him again."

"Not for a while," I said as she released my hand. "I'll see this business through to the end. I think it's about time I started turning over a few rocks."

"Not yet," she said quickly. "Not until you have to. The time will come soon enough."

So we waited. Kate was right. The time did come sooner than we expected. One evening a fellow who called himself Jojo Birney rode into the valley about supper time and asked Mrs. Horton to put him up a few days. I was uneasy the moment I laid eyes on him, although he was the most unassuming of all men, small, bald-headed, and watery-eyed. His mount was a fine, black gelding that showed he had been ridden hard, so I guessed somebody had been chasing him. He did not wear a gun. His clothes were the usual range garb, but he was in no way a cowboy.

"It will cost you fifty dollars a day," Mrs. Horton said.

Birney blinked as if surprised, wiped a hand across his face as if he wasn't sure he could stand the freight, then nodded, saying: "That's a mite higher than I expected, but I'm hungry, I'm tired, and I can't run any more for a while. I'll stay here two, three days and rest up."

He gave Mrs. Horton five double eagles and took a chair at the table without being asked. We had almost finished everything, but there was always some left over. Whatever any of us thought about Mrs. Horton, we couldn't accuse her of being stingy with the food she put on the table, but, when Birney got done, there wasn't a smidgen left in any of the bowls.

I couldn't see a thing about this beaten-down, scared

little man that should have worried me, but I couldn't shake off the uneasy feeling I had about him. I realized it was a matter of intuition more than logic, but the feeling grew as I sat there watching him, noticing how his eyes kept turning to Kate.

There was nothing to be alarmed about, Kate being the good-looking girl that she was. Chances were Birney hadn't seen many pretty girls lately. I also was aware that I was jumpy because I had been expecting an assassin to show up. Landon wouldn't quit trying if what Kate had said about him was true, and I had no reason to doubt her. This was not a good hiding place for Kate because Landon would guess she had come here, but, whenever I suggested that she go somewhere else, she got a stubborn look in her eyes and shook her head, saying this was the only place she could go.

When Birney finished eating, he stood up, pushed back his chair, then slid it into place again. He said: "I'm going to take care of my horse. He's come a long ways today and he's as tired as I am. I've been hunted like an animal, but I gave 'em the slip." He shrugged. "They just wanted me out of the country anyhow, but I'll be moving on soon as I rest up."

"Who's they?" Mrs. Horton asked.

"Some men who are trying to grab all the land there is on the Gunnison that'll grow hay," he said bitterly. "They kept pushing me until I finally shot and killed a deputy. They own the law up there, you know, so I had to get out." He yawned, then said: "I'll go to bed right away if you'll tell me where."

"Second cabin from the house," Mrs. Horton said. "You'll have it to yourself. We never hold a meal for no-body, Mister Birney. If you want to eat in the morning, you'd best pop out of bed when you hear the triangle."

"I like to eat," he said. "I'll be here."

He started toward the front room, then turned when Mrs. Horton asked: "How'd you hear about my place?"

He hesitated, staring at the floor and scratching a boot toe across the braided rug he was standing on. "Well, ma'am, let's just say I've got some friends who stop and see me once in a while. They told me about it. They ain't ones to stand still very long with a rope hanging over their heads, but they did say you could cook up the best grub there was on this side of the mountains."

After he left, there was silence for a moment, then Mrs. Horton said: "He's lying. There ain't no trouble on the Gunnison like that or I'd have heard of it."

"I don't like it," I said.

"Neither do I," Smith agreed.

Mrs. Horton seemed surprised. "I figure he had his own reasons for lying, but, if you think that little half-pint would harm Kate, you've been eating loco weed. He just ain't the kind of hardcase who usually stops here."

"Then I've been eating loco weed," Smith said. "Seemed to me he overplayed his part. He's a killer, the sneaky kind who puts a knife into your back."

The Kid hadn't said a word, but now he nodded. "You know, John, I hadn't thought of it, but you're right. I never liked knife-fighters. They're all sneaky."

Kate had been watching me uneasily. "I don't think he's the kind of man who would hurt me, or the kind Max would hire."

"It's all a bunch of hogwash, honey," Mrs. Horton said. "Now don't you worry your purty head about that little runt."

"You both sleep upstairs?" I asked.

Mrs. Horton nodded. "My room's next to Kate's. If he

got into the house and came upstairs, I'd hear him before he got to Kate's room."

"No, you wouldn't, Aunt Becky," Kate said quickly. "Not if it was in the middle of the night. The way you sleep, it would take an earthquake to wake you up."

Mrs. Horton was a woman of fixed opinions, but now I saw doubt flow across her face. "Yeah, I reckon you're right, honey. I'd never forgive myself if that little bastard sneaked into your room and stuck a knife into you while I was snoring away." She glared at me. "You're the big cheese of your outfit. Got any ideas?"

"I have," Kate said. "I told Del I'd feel easier if he was sleeping with me, but Del said you'd never stand for it."

Mrs. Horton was shocked, then I was surprised to see her smile. "He's dead right. You can't be that scared."

"Is there a room directly across the hall from Kate's?" I asked.

Mrs. Horton nodded. "I don't like that notion, neither. I don't want none of you men sleeping in the house right across from Kate."

That made me sore. I was always kind of sore at her anyway, mostly on general principles. I said: "Well, by God, Missus Horton, what do you think we are? She hired us to protect her."

"Which same don't mean you wouldn't take advantage of her," Mrs. Horton snarled, "particularly since it appears she wants to be taken advantage of."

"We had plenty of chances when we were bringing her here," I said, holding onto my temper so I wouldn't get up and wallop her across the face. "Maybe you'd like to sit up with her all night, though I sure wouldn't trust you to stay awake."

Kate was red in the face, as angry as I had ever seen her,

but she handled herself very well in not letting Mrs. Horton see how angry she was. "If they want to sit up all night to watch out for my safety, I'm certainly going to let them. Otherwise, I'll sleep in the bunkhouse with them."

"Oh, no, honey, I can't let you do that," Mrs. Horton said quickly. "I tell you what I will agree to." She nodded at me. "You and Smith can split the night." She stabbed a forefinger in the Kid's direction. "But not him. He stays out of the house at night."

I figured the Kid would blow up in her face, but he surprised me by laughing. "You sure got me pegged right, old woman. You don't trust me, and I sure as hell didn't trust you from the first morning I sat down here to eat breakfast. I figger you'd sell Kate out to this Landon *hombre* for five cents if you had the chance."

Mrs. Horton began to shake with ill-suppressed fury. She rose, her chin trembling. "You sneaky little whippersnapper! I'm going to boot you out of this house on your. . . ."

"No, Aunt Becky." Kate grabbed an arm and shook it. "It's all my fault for bringing them here, but you can't blame him for what he said. You insulted him first."

For a moment Mrs. Horton stood glaring at the Kid, one hand coming up to rub a mole on the right side of her chin. "I reckon I did at that," she said, "but what I said still holds. You ain't coming into the house at night."

"Suits me," the Kid said indifferently. "I ain't anxious to lose a night's sleep."

Mrs. Horton ignored him after that. She nodded at me. "Now just how are you gonna work it?"

"John can take it till midnight," I said. "I'll take the rest of the night. We'll leave the door open enough to keep an eye on Kate's room. John will come in right after dark and go up to the room. If Birney sees him, he won't think anything of it, with him coming in that early. I'll come in through the back door at midnight and feel my way up the stairs. John can feel his way back down. We won't light a lamp."

Mrs. Horton nodded. "Just so I'll know what to figure on."

"I have the first room to the right at the head of the stairs," Kate said.

"We'll find it," I said.

As soon as we were outside, the Kid said: "Now ain't she a bitch?" He glanced at me. "What are you gonna do, Del?"

"If this Birney is what we think he is," I said, "I'm going after Landon. He's bound to show up sooner or later."

"I'm riding out in the morning," he said. "I'll see you in town."

He strode on across the yard to the corral. Smith said: "I've been expecting him to pull out. He's stayed longer than I expected."

I nodded and went into our cabin, knowing there was no use to argue with the Kid after what Mrs. Horton had said. I didn't blame him. I might have done the same thing.

# Chapter Eleven

I got out of bed shortly after midnight to relieve Smith. The inside of the house was as black as the inside of a cave, so I had to feel my way across the kitchen to the stairs, then up the stairs to the hall. When I reached it, I called—"John."—thinking he might decide I was Birney and start shooting.

"Here," he said.

I worked my way along the hall until I reached the door of the room where John was waiting. I asked: "Quiet?"

"Like a graveyard," he answered.

A nearly full moon was riding high in the sky, and enough light filtered into the room for me to see him sitting in a chair just inside the door. He got up and yawned, saying: "I hate to miss half a night's sleep. You sure this is necessary?"

"Yeah, I'm sure," I said. "If he doesn't show up tonight, he will tomorrow night."

"All right," he said, and yawned again. "I'll try to catch up on my sleep tomorrow."

"We'd better," I said, "if we have to do it again tomorrow night. Be careful going through the house. It's dark as a bull's gut."

"I've got eyes like an owl," he said, and disappeared down the hall.

I heard him on the stairs, then a few minutes later heard him bang into the kitchen table, and, swearing at him under my breath, hoped the racket didn't wake Kate or Mrs. Horton. *Eyes like an owl!* I thought sourly. I listened, but I

96

didn't hear Kate or Mrs. Horton stir, so I decided Smith hadn't done any damage.

I got through the night, but it seemed to go on and on. I ate breakfast with Kate and Mrs. Horton. The Kid came in before we were finished, sat without saying a word, ate, and left. Smith did not show up, and I didn't blame him. I aimed to go to bed as soon as I got to the bunkhouse, but it didn't quite work that way.

When I'd finished my third cup of coffee, Kate said: "I don't think you need to stay up again tonight, Del. It's more than I have a right to ask you to do. Besides, I still don't think Birney is the kind who'd hurt a fly."

"That's exactly the reason he may be very good at killing," I said. "Men who are killers often don't look like killers."

Mrs. Horton looked at me as if she agreed with what I'd said, and that just about killed her. She said, reluctantly I thought: "You're all right, Del. The worst man who ever stayed here was a little, dried-up runt we called Louie. He had a squeaky voice and lisped, and you had to feel kind of sorry for him, being so helpless-looking and all." She shook her head, scowling. "You know, after he left I heard he had killed two whores in Cripple Creek by cutting them up into little pieces. I'd say you better watch again tonight. I can kick Birney out, but he'd sneak back into the valley after dark, so I wouldn't be doing no good."

"Let him stay," I said.

I met Birney coming in just as I left. He said—"Good morning."—in a pleasant voice, and went on into the house. I stood on the porch a moment, staring at his back as he crossed the front room to the kitchen, wondering if my fears were justified, then I went on, knowing I'd have to sit up as long as Birney was there, or even longer.

The Kid was saddling up as I crossed the yard. I hesitated, thinking I shouldn't urge him to stay, feeling the way he did. I knew it wouldn't do any good anyway, but, when he looked up and saw me, he called: "Del, come here!"

He had mounted by the time I reached him. I said: "You won't change your mind?"

I thought he expected me to say it, but he just grinned and shook his head. "I've had enough of that old biddy and then some." He scowled, and added: "You know, Del, I've met some ornery, low-down, mean women . . . I don't think much of women anyhow, though Kate does seem to be different . . . but Missus Horton now . . . she's the prize as far as I'm concerned, and you couldn't pay me enough to stay."

"Kate owes you some money," I said, "but she won't be able to pay you for a while."

"I figger she's good for it," he said. "I'll see you in Rolly in a day or two. Chances are Kate'll be there, too."

"She'll have to be," I said, "but, before she goes, I'm riding into Rolly to have a talk with that Judge Bailey she's mentioned. I don't see any reason to put off reading the will and getting the estate settled no matter what Landon does."

"What I called you over for was to tell you that you've got plenty of reason to keep your eyes on Birney," the Kid said. "I was purty sore last night when the old bitch thought I couldn't be trusted to help guard Kate, so I figgered I'd make myself useful by staying up and watching Birney's cabin. After you left, I pulled on my boots and sneaked outside. I guess I'd been there about an hour when he came out of his cabin and started toward the house, slipping along easy-like, but he must have spotted me. I was fool enough to light a smoke, so I figure he smelled it. Anyhow, he stopped and stood looking around and listening for a minute or two, then he went back into his cabin and shut the door."

"I'm not surprised," I said. "He probably decided it wasn't the right night."

"I reckon," the Kid agreed. "He didn't come out of the cabin like a man who had a good reason for being out there. He was just too damned careful." He raised a hand. "I'll see you in two, three days."

"Where are you going," I asked, "in case we need you?"

"Dunno," he said, "but I'll show up in time to give you a hand."

I watched him ride away, thinking he had something in mind, but didn't want me to know what it was. I turned toward our cabin, thinking about Birney. I couldn't discount what the Kid had told me, although I realized it might not mean a thing. I pulled off my boots and lay down on my bunk, and didn't know anything until I woke just before noon and found Smith sitting on his bunk and yawning.

"Time to put the feedbag on," Smith said. "I never slept this long before in my life."

"The Kid's gone," I said, and mentioned what he'd seen Birney do the night before.

"I'm not surprised," Smith said. "A man gets a feeling about a gent like Birney, and mine's not good."

"Neither's mine," I said. "I keep telling myself we're scared, and maybe seeing something in him that's not there."

"I know," Smith agreed, "but we can't take a chance, so we'll have to sit up again tonight."

Dinner was on the table when we reached the kitchen. Birney was ahead of us. He said: "I'm glad you jaspers are here. Missus Horton says we're waiting a couple of minutes, but my tapeworm's been telling me it's a long two minutes."

Kate sat beside me, and, after we had filled our plates, she reached over and took my hand and squeezed it. I was afraid that she or Mrs. Horton would say something about our sitting up, forgetting for the moment that Birney wasn't supposed to know anything about it. If we didn't trap him in the act, we wouldn't know about him for sure, and, unless we found out for sure, we wouldn't know if Landon was still trying to kill Kate, or whether we should be watching for another killer to show up.

After dinner I got busy with the bucksaw, and Smith took over the Kid's job with the livestock. As soon as Kate finished washing the dishes, she came out to sit on an upended block and watched me for a few minutes. When I had sawed enough to last until the next day, I tossed the bucksaw toward the pile of wood and sat down beside her.

"Kate," I said, "we can't go on wondering what Landon is figuring on next, so I'm going into Rolly and have a talk with your friend, Judge Bailey. He's got to read the will and get Landon off your ranch."

She seemed to withdraw into herself when I said that, her mouth began to quiver, and then she started to cry. I felt guilty as hell because I know how she felt, and I wondered if I was doing the wrong thing to keep scaring her. I didn't think so. She was refusing to face reality, but she had to sooner or later, and it had better be now than later. She couldn't go on hiding out here.

I moved closer to her and put an arm around her. "We've got to talk about it, Kate."

She pressed against me and finally stopped crying, then sat dabbing at her eyes before she could say: "I know you think I'm a crybaby, but I've never been like this before. Daddy tried to raise me to be tough like a boy, you know, grit your teeth and bear it, but this time I just can't do it. I guess you're the only friend I have who can do anything for me, but, when I think of you getting killed on my account, I just go to pieces."

100

"I'm not going to get killed," I said. "Landon doesn't know anything about me. I can handle him if I can get him alone, so I'll go out to the Diamond M in the middle of the day. If I'm lucky, his crew won't be around."

She was silent for a while, then she said slowly: "All right, Del. If you think that's what you have to do, then go ahead, but remember one thing. I want you alive. Getting the Diamond M is second."

"I'll remember that." I told her about the Kid, that he wasn't running out on her, that he just couldn't stand Mrs. Horton any longer, then I added: "He promised me he'd be in Rolly when we needed him."

She nodded. "Aunt Becky can be a holy terror, and she always is when she takes a dislike to someone. She didn't like the Kid from the first. She said she smelled outlaw all over him. She's had too many men like him here, she said, and she's afraid of them. Says you can't trust them."

"She's partly right," I said, "but he's been a good friend to me and John. The Kid told me he didn't think much of women, but he liked you."

I thought that was going to start her crying again, but it didn't. She dabbed at her eyes and was silent for a moment, then said: "I couldn't ask for more than that, could I?"

"Not from him," I said. "The world is made up of two kinds of people, the ones he likes and the ones he hates, and there's no one in between."

She stared at the wooden ridge across the creek for a long time, before she said: "I never thought in the years I was growing up and the years I've been away that I would ever live like this. I've just never been so scared before. Every night, when I go to sleep, I wonder if I'll wake up in the morning." She hesitated as if completely satisfied to sit here with me forever, but finally she rose and said reluctantly: "I'd better go in and help Aunt Becky with supper."

Supper was much like dinner, Birney trying to be pleasant and disarming, with the rest of us too tense even to carry on a conversation. Smith and I returned to our cabin, and a short time later we saw Birney go into his. Later Smith slipped out into the darkness and started his vigil in the house. At midnight I took his place. He left the room, saying that, if Birney didn't make his move tonight, we'd better work him over in the morning until he told us why he was really here, that we didn't swallow the story he'd told. I agreed, not sure that was the right thing to do, but knowing we had to make something happen. We couldn't go on waiting for the second shoe to fall.

As on the previous night, I sat just inside the room across the hall from Kate's room, leaving my door wide open. An hour passed, maybe two. I had no judgment of time, but each minute seemed to run on and on into an eternity.

I guess I had dropped off to sleep because I came to with a start, my right hand instinctively dropping to my gun and lifting it from leather. I realized at once that the slight noise that woke me was the sound of Kate's door being opened.

I was on my feet at once and easing across the hall, cursing myself for dropping off to sleep. The window in Kate's room was about three feet to the left of the head of her bed. The thin light coming through the window was enough for me to make out the shadowy form of a man bending over her, a knife raised above her body poised for a downward stroke. I fired, and fired again as he started to go down.

Kate sat up and began to scream. The first slug had slammed the man away from the bed and back against the wall. I was on him at once, not knowing how hard he was hit. In the night light, I still couldn't tell, but he wasn't moving, so I struck a match and lighted the lamp that was on the stand beside the bed.

Birney was lying on his back, a bullet hole in his chest. Apparently my second shot had missed completely. He wasn't dead, but he didn't have much life left. Blood was pouring out of his wound, and his mouth sagged open, his face the pallor of death.

Kneeling beside him, I asked: "Who hired you?"

His lips moved, but I barely heard the words: "Landon. He's safe, and I'm dying. He had the money to hire me. That's the way it . . . always . . . goes."

He died, his unseeing eyes staring at the ceiling, his mouth still open. Mrs. Horton had rushed into the room and now stood motionless, wide-eyed, staring at Birney's body. Kate was sitting up and crying in long, breathless sobs. I had not been aware she had stopped screaming. I sat down beside her on the bed and, putting an arm around her, held her close as she gradually stopped crying.

When Kate finally caught her breath, she whispered: "That's the third time, Del. The third time you've saved my life. Is it ever going to end?"

"It will," I said, "I promise."

Smith had come in and, looking at the body, said: "I guess we figured him right."

"Get his carcass out of here," Mrs. Horton snapped. "Put him on the bed in the room across the hall."

Smith lifted the body and carried it out of Kate's room.

Mrs. Horton said: "Honey, you're going to sleep with me the rest of the night. You ain't gonna stay in here by yourself."

Still Kate clung to me as if she's rather have me with her than Mrs. Horton, but I didn't point that out to the old woman. Kate felt safe in my arms, and I had a hunch she wouldn't feel safe anywhere else even with Birney dead. I pried Kate's arms apart and stood up, figuring that Mrs. Horton had her mind made up, and, once that happened, nothing would change it.

"We'll talk tomorrow, Kate," I said.

I left the house with Smith. When we were outside, I told him what Birney had said just before he died, then added: "I don't think Kate heard him, so it would be my word against Landon's if he was tried, which I figure he never would be in this county."

"But now we know for sure," Smith said. "It's just been Kate's notion up till now. Maybe the judge will believe you."

"But a jury wouldn't," I said. "I'm leaving tomorrow. You can look after Kate."

"Going to beard the lion in his den?"

"Something like that," I said.

"The lion may have bigger teeth than you figure on," Smith said.

"I don't think so," I said. "It's not much of a lion who hires men to murder a woman."

"Put that lion with his back against the wall," Smith said, "and you'll get a different view of his teeth."

That was right. I was aware of it all the way down to the bottom of my guts, but I knew what I had to do, and I had to do it alone. The Kid was gone, and I couldn't take Smith with me because I didn't dare leave Kate here without some protection. That made me think pretty hard about me, and her, and I knew then I loved her. It was the first time I had been aware of that, but I was now. There was no halfway point for me from here on.

# Chapter Twelve

If it had been left up to me, I'd have thrown Birney's body outside for the coyotes to chew on. I figured that was the best he deserved, but Mrs. Horton, tough as she was, would have no part of it.

"He was a human being," she said as soon as we finished breakfast. "Not much of a one, but he still deserves a Christian burial. There's a little graveyard on the slope to the north. My husband is buried there along with four others who died while they were staying here. You men find shovels and dig a grave. We'll bury the bastard this afternoon."

Grave-digging was not my favorite line of work, but I had no intention of arguing with Mrs. Horton. I glanced at Smith, who grimaced and then nodded, so I drank the rest of my coffee and rose. Kate had not come down for breakfast, so I asked about her.

"She had a hell of a night just like you'd expect," Mrs. Horton answered, "but she'll be all right. Trouble is, she thinks Max will still find a way to kill her."

"Not if I kill him first," I said. "As soon as we finish the burying, I'm heading for Rolly."

"Somebody's got to," Mrs. Horton said grimly, "or Max will hire a man who can get the job done. Birney was an idiot. He could have found a better way than trying to knife her in bed."

"It's my guess that was the kind of jayhoo he was," I said. "A knife man doesn't like to use anything else, so he had to do it at night."

*"Hmmph,"* Mrs. Horton sniffed. "I still say he was an idiot."

We found shovels and took along a couple of picks in case we hit any hardpan. The graveyard was about a quarter of a mile up the slope above the buildings. It was surrounded by a barbed-wire fence, and the graves were in good condition; the grass on each had been clipped, the weeds pulled, and there was a dried-up bouquet of columbines on one.

The wooden markers were weathered so much it was hard to read the names, but the one where the flowers were held the words—**Henry Horton**—so I judged that had to be Mrs. Horton's husband's grave. I found I was finally gaining a little more respect for Mrs. Horton. As hard-bitten as she was, she had a human side that she kept well-hidden, but I saw it in her feeling for Kate, and now it was evident she had respected and loved her dead husband. The thought occurred to me that someday she would be buried beside him, but there would be no one to cut the grass and pull the weeds.

Smith and I selected a spot as far removed from the other graves as we could, thinking he must have been the worst of the lot and didn't deserve any company. Grinning, Smith said: "We can't have him contaminating the rest of them."

The ground was hard, and we hit some large rocks that took time to dislodge. We decided we weren't doing the perfect job a man could take pride in, but we weren't concerned about that. We just wanted to get it done. By noon the grave was three feet deep, and, as we walked back to the house for dinner, we agreed it would take most of the afternoon to finish it, which meant I'd have to wait until morning to leave for Rolly.

Before we reached the house, Smith said: "You're getting a mite fond of Kate, aren't you?"

I had a notion to tell him it was none of his business, but smothered the impulse. John Smith was not a man to talk to in that manner. In the weeks I had known him, I had learned to respect and like him, and I had no doubt he'd be with me at the finish, if it came to a gun fight with Max Landon and the Diamond M crew.

"I am," I said. "It's kind of funny, too, with me thinking for a while I just wanted to get her off my back and get to hell out of here, but, damn it, she's the kind of girl who grows on you. I think she's a lot stronger than she seems to be because of the trouble she's been in ever since we've known her."

"She's scared out of her boots," Smith said, "which sure is understandable. I think you're right. She acts like a clinging vine, but I don't think she is." He grinned a little in the self-deprecating way he had, and added: "She's my kind of woman, but I'm too old for her. I'd make a try, though, if you weren't going to."

"Nobody's keeping you from trying," I said, surprised and a little nettled to learn he felt that way.

"Oh, yes, there is," he said. "You are, whether you aim to do it or not. You've got a lead on me I'd never make up. It's my guess she's had plenty of men chasing her, but she's been hard to catch up to the time she met you. You got into her life at just the right time."

I remembered what she'd said about her father's keeping boys away from her when she'd been growing up and thought that Smith was probably right. My mother often talked about some of the old maids around Prairie City who kept trying too hard, and a man never wanted a woman who threw herself at him, but it was different with

Kate. I understood how she felt. She made it plain the instant I entered the kitchen, running to me and hugging me.

"Three times," she said. "Three times I would have been killed if it hadn't been for you. I can't ever repay you."

"Don't try," Mrs. Horton snapped.

For once I was glad to hear what the old woman had to say. I hugged Kate as hard as she hugged me, saying: "Forget it. I've got something to say to you, when it's the right time, and paying me back is not part of it."

She tipped her head back and smiled. "I hope I know what it is," she said.

"Quit your lallygagging and sit down and rest," Mrs. Horton said brusquely.

We did. As I ate, I glanced at Kate who picked at her food, looking at me now and then, but staring at her plate most of the time. Her eyes were red, her hair was not as neatly brushed and pinned as it usually was, and she looked very tired. *She can't go on this way,* I thought.

As I walked back to the graveyard with Smith, he said: "Kate's about had it. You think she'll give in to Landon?"

"No," I answered. "She might have a nervous breakdown or go out of her mind or something like that, but, as long as she's able to control herself, I don't think she'll give up."

Smith nodded. "That's the way I pegged her, too."

We hit a patch of hardpan and had to use our picks. That slowed us up, and by five o'clock we were still not down six feet. I stopped work and leaned on the shovel handle, saying: "What do you think, John?"

"I think we've gone deep enough for that son-of-a-bitch," he said. "There's no law that says a grave has to be six feet deep."

That was when I saw Mr. Horton and Kate coming up the slope in a wagon. I said: "Maybe Missus Horton thinks the same. It's my guess she's fetching the body now."

Smith nodded and climbed out of the grave. "If she wants a deeper grave, she can dig it herself."

"She won't," I said, as I tossed the shovel to the ground and scrambled up beside him.

When Mrs. Horton and Kate reached us, I saw that my guess was right. The body was wrapped in a piece of canvas and lay in the bed of the wagon. I said: "We hit some hard digging and didn't get the grave six feet down like it's supposed to be."

She stepped out of the wagon seat to the ground, looked into the grave, and nodded. "Deep enough," she said. "You can drop him into it."

Birney was not a heavy man, but still it must have been a chore for the women to carry him down the stairs and lift him into the wagon. I regretted that Smith and I had not thought about doing it before we left the house after dinner, but I had expected to have the grave finished before this and that we'd be back to the house before it was necessary to move the body. I didn't ask, but I figured that Mrs. Horton had not wanted to put the burial off another day.

Smith and I each took an end of the canvas-wrapped corpse and dropped it into the grave, not too gently, either. There seemed to be a kind of insanity about going to all this trouble for a man who had tried to murder Kate. I picked up the shovel and would have started throwing dirt into the grave, if Mrs. Horton had not opened a worn Bible.

She read several verses in a loud voice as if she thought God was deaf—the Twenty-Third Psalm, the Lord's Prayer, and a few others—then she closed the Bible and, looking up at the sky, said: "Lord, this man we're burying is the most complete son-of-a-bitch I ever met, and I have wide experience with that breed of Your creation. We know You can forgive him, and we also know You punish men like him for their evil-doing, so we leave him in Your hands. Amen." She turned to Kate and said gruffly: "Let's get back to the house. I'll put a head board up later."

Smith leaned on his shovel and watched them drive away, then he said: "That old woman is the most surprising female I ever met. Sometimes I almost like her."

"It's hard," I said, and began shoveling dirt into the grave.

We finished not long after the sun was down, and then trudged back down the slope to the barn where we left the shovels and picks. We were tired and hungry and dirty, but Mrs. Horton had kept our suppers warm, saying, when we went into the kitchen, that she thought we'd want to finish.

When we were done eating, Mrs. Horton looked directly at me as she said: "You're heading for Rolly in the morning?"

It was more of a statement than a question, and I resented it because I thought she was giving an order rather than asking my intentions. I said: "That's right."

Kate stared at me, her face very pale. Her coffee cup shook in her hand as she picked it up and lifted it to her lips, then she said in a low tone: "Are you sure that is the right thing to do?"

"It's the only thing I can do," I said. "John will look after you. Don't take any chances. Landon won't know for a while that his latest scheme failed, but, when he finds it out, he'll find another man, maybe someone who will try to dry-gulch you from the brush along the creek, so you'd better stay inside the house."

"I'll be careful," she said.

"I'll see that she does," Mrs. Horton said. "Now I've got to admit that you two men have been earning your pay, but

110

I'll tell you I didn't think much of the lot of you, with Kate just kind of falling into your company the way she done. Looks like you aim to see it through. What do you figure to do when you get to Rolly?"

I turned to Kate. "Who can I trust?"

"Judge Bailey," she said quickly, then paused as she thought about it, then she added: "I'm not sure who else. You see, when I got to Rolly this summer, I didn't talk to anyone except the judge. I was tired after riding in the stagecoach all the way from Durango, so, when I got my hotel room, I went right to bed. I used to know the Rolly folks pretty well, but folks change. Now with Max sitting in the driver's seat, he can scare any of them into either not talking to you or lying." She hesitated, tapping a fingertip on the table. "I did have a lot of friends in Rolly when Daddy was alive and before I went away to school. Maybe they're still friends, men like the banker, Adam Jessup, and the preacher, Charlie Nathrop. I suppose there are others. I just don't know how much they've changed."

"I'll talk to the judge first," I said. "I'll ask him to set up a date to read the will. I guess you can go to town any day for that."

She stared at her dirty plate for a moment before she said: "Yes, but I just don't know if I can face Max or not. The judge will want him to be there, when the will's read. I'm pretty sure he's in it, but I don't know how it's worded, and that makes all the difference in the world."

"I'll be with you, when it's read, if you want me to be there," I said.

"Of course I want you to be there," she said gratefully, "and you tell the judge I said so."

I didn't press her for more information because I didn't think she could tell me anything else, and also because I knew I had to feel my way and play everything by ear. Kate trusted the judge completely, so I had to go on the basis that I could, too, regardless of how much he trusted me.

Before I left the house that evening, I told Kate I didn't know when I would be back, but I'd make it just as soon as I could because there was no sense in wasting time now. I regretted letting it go as long as we had, but Kate had wanted it that way, and with Birney showing up it was a good thing I was still here.

Besides, the days before Birney had ridden in had been good days, and they had given me a chance to know Kate and to discover how I felt about her. I hugged her and kissed her before I left the house, and thought about telling her I loved her, but I didn't because it would only make it worse, if I didn't come back, and I knew the odds were that I wouldn't.

All that Kate said was: "Come back, Del. Nothing else matters."

Mrs. Horton had breakfast ready in the morning, when I went into the kitchen, the day barely started with the pale light of dawn showing above the timbered ridge line to the east. I saddled up, and, by the time I reached the main road along the river, the sun was just tipping into sight.

I had looked back once at the house where Kate was sleeping, or hoped she had recovered enough from the scare Birney's attack had given her to sleep. I wondered how so many things could have happened in the few days since I had walked past her hotel room and heard her scream for help. Time, I knew, could never be measured by days and weeks, but, rather, by events. Now it was important for me to come back for Kate's sake as well as my own.

# Chapter Thirteen

I reached Rolly before noon, put my horse in the livery stable, and took a room in the hotel because I was sure I'd be in Rolly at least for the one night. I washed up and went downstairs to the dining room for dinner. I had thought about what I would say to Judge Bailey all the way into town, but I still didn't know exactly how I'd approach it.

According to Kate, Bailey was honest and decent and kind, and a friend, but, now that I was here, I was reluctant to see him. I supposed it was because I didn't fully trust Kate's judgment. She had been out of the country a great deal the last four years, and, as she had said last night, people change. Judge Bailey might be as scared of Max Landon as anyone else. Another reason I was reluctant to see him was the fact that I was a wanted man, and talking to the judge who represented the law was going to be a nerve-wracking experience, but nerve-wracking or not, I had, as Mrs. Horton put it, to see it through.

When I finished eating, I went outside, the sun astonishingly hot for this altitude. I stood for a moment looking along the street. Nothing had changed. Rolly still looked like a ghost town, most of the buildings deserted, their windows boarded up, and no one was on the street except a drunk who was sleeping peacefully in the shadow of the Mercantile, one of the few businesses in town that was still operating.

I told myself there was no sense in putting this off, so I crossed the street to the bank building and climbed the outside stairs to the second floor that held a number of offices. Kate had told me where Bailey's office was, so it took me only a moment to locate it.

I opened the door, and I stepped inside. A small man sat at a desk, his face as wrinkled as the prunes we used to have for breakfast when I rode for Wineglass in Montana. He wore thick glasses, and, when he looked up from the law book he was reading, he blinked a moment before I came into focus for him. At least, I thought it was that way because he stared at me for several seconds before he said a word. I suppose he couldn't make out whether I was a stranger or someone he knew, and I think he was surprised when he figured out I was a stranger.

"What can I do for you?" he asked finally.

I had remained just inside the doorway and didn't say a word until after he had spoken. Of course, I couldn't tell by looking at him how honest or decent he was, or how good a friend of Kate's he was, or how much Max Landon had cowed him, but one thing was sure. Whatever I did in Rolly had to start with him.

I wasn't impressed as I walked toward his desk. He seemed too frail to be outside in a strong wind without risking his life, and I was reminded of Kate's words that none of her friends in Rolly could stand up to Landon.

When I reached his desk, I held out my hand and said: "My name's Delaney." It was the first time I had told anyone my last name since I had left Prairie City, but I knew he wouldn't be satisfied with anything else. Anyhow, I didn't think that one of the reward dodgers bearing my name would have reached an area so far from home.

He rose and shook hands with me, saying: "Pleased to meet you. I'm Judge Bailey."

His grip was firm, but his hand was so thin it was almost

114

claw-like, and the back was covered by liver spots. I couldn't guess his age, but everything about Judge Bailey indicated a lot of years. He motioned to a chair.

I saw no point in wasting time, so I said: "Are you interested in Kate Muldoon's whereabouts?"

He had been sitting back in his chair, but, when I asked that, he jumped up as suddenly as if he found himself sitting on a tack, his face alive with interest. "By God, yes," he shouted. "Do you know where she is?"

"I know," I answered. "Max Landon knows, too. The question is . . . can you or the sheriff or anyone else in Rolly protect her from him?"

For one brief moment it seemed as if twenty years had been stripped from his thin, wrinkled face, then the expression fled, and he dropped back into his chair, a beaten old man. He said: "No." He leaned forward, and, picking up a meerschaum pipe that had been darkened by years of smoking, filled it from a can of Prince Albert, and tamped the tobacco down, his faded blue eyes pinned on me. He asked: "Is she well?"

"Outside of being scared to death," I answered, "she's fine. Landon has tried to kill her three times."

He leaned back in his swivel chair and fished for a match in a vest pocket. His hand trembled as he lighted his pipe. He shook the flame out, pulled on his pipe, and blew out a cloud of smoke. He kept watching me through the smoke and must have decided I'd pass, because he asked: "What's your connection with Kate?"

"I was staying in the hotel the night the first attempt was made on her life," I said. "I had the room across the hall from her and heard her scream. I kicked the door in and pulled a man off her who was trying to smother her with a pillow."

"I see," he said. "When she attempted to leave town, another man tried to shoot her, and you killed him?"

The tone was definitely a question. I nodded, saying: "That's the size of it. The third attempt on her life was made where she's hiding out. A man tried to knife her in the middle of the night. Before he died, he said Landon had hired him to kill her. Until then she'd had no evidence against Landon, but this fellow lived long enough to name him."

"Did anybody else hear him?"

"I don't think so."

He shook his head. "Then if it came to trial, it would be his word against yours, and in this county a stranger's word isn't worth a damn." He puffed steadily on his pipe, his sharp little eyes pinned on my face. I squirmed in my chair, feeling like a bug under a microscope. Finally he asked: "Did Kate tell you how things stack up in this county?"

"Yes," I answered, "she said she'd been gone for a year and didn't know how folks felt since her father died. She said she used to have a lot of friends here, but she knows people change."

"She's right," he said, and then he asked: "Just who the hell are you?"

"A drifter," I said. "Riding though the country looking for a job. I happened to be at the right place at the right time to save Kate's life. I was traveling with two friends, and Kate has hired us as bodyguards."

"She paying you well?"

"One hundred dollars a day," I said. "That suits us, though she says she can't pay until the estate is settled."

"That's right," he agreed. "Tell me something. How far are you and your friends willing to go to earn that kind of money?"

"As far as necessary," I answered. "From what Kate says, it strikes me that she will never get her inheritance until Max Landon is dead."

"Correct," he said, "and that is a hell of a thing for a judge to say."

He rose and walked to a window where he stood staring down into the street, a somber and, I thought, a bitter old man. He said without turning: "Max Landon is the law hereabouts. The sheriff is a man who goes with the winning side, and right now that's Landon. He's the only law man in the county, and he sure as hell won't get any help from the neighboring counties. Or from the state, either. As far as most people who live here go, there just aren't many of us any more. When it comes down to use of force, we're not able to buck Landon. It would be like a child going up against a grown man. Sure, we could die trying, but to what purpose?"

It seemed to me that Bailey was simply corroborating what Kate had told me, but it was different, coming from a man who was supposed to uphold the law and deal out justice to the citizens of the county. He was deeply ashamed, I thought. Perhaps he had even considered picking up a gun himself to enforce the law, but, as he had just said, to what purpose? I couldn't really fault the old man.

He turned to face me, still pulling on his pipe. "Kate may not have told you some facts which are very pertinent. Her father, Red Muldoon, was a big, two-fisted Irishman who, in his time, ran everything in the county, back to the days when Rolly was a boom town and the mines were going great guns. He wanted a boy, but he got Kate. There was nothing he could do about that, although, God knows, he tried to make a boy out of her. Instead, she turned out to be a hell of a fine girl, as you probably know by now. When

Red finally found out he couldn't change nature, he shipped her off to school.

"Max Landon had showed up before that, and he knew how to toady after Red, so Red got to thinking a lot about him. Some of the rest of us could see that Max was as slick as a coyote, but Red fastened the love he would have given a boy of his own on Max. Not that he didn't love Kate, and blood was always very important to Red, but the fact remained that he raised Max to run the Diamond M after he died."

Bailey returned to his desk and sat down. His pipe had gone out, and he laid it on the ashtray, then wiped a hand across his face. "I've always been Red's lawyer, but I never told him a thing in his life. Nobody did. He'd tell me what he wanted, and it was up to me to do it. The will he left is his creation. I can't tell you what's in it, but I can say it is the damnedest will I ever saw in all my years of being a lawyer. What nails my hide to the barn door is the fact that there was never anything I could do about it."

"Kate said the will was supposed to be read the day after Landon tried to have her killed," I said.

"That's right," he agreed. "I don't suppose you want to tell me where she is?"

"No," I said.

"It doesn't matter," he said. "I'd be afraid for her to come back to Rolly just yet anyhow. Of course, none of us knew what had happened to her, but I think all of us were afraid Landon had murdered her." He leaned forward, eyes pinned on me again. "I have no way of knowing how tough a man you are, Delaney. It's hard for me to believe that any man who hires out his gun as you're doing would risk his life fighting a man like Max Landon. He's not like Red, though old Red didn't know that. Red was tough as an old

118

mossyhorn, but he was a man of principle, and Max has only one principle . . . me first."

"I've never figured I was a tough hand," I said. "I've always been a cowboy, but seems like lately I've been into some pretty tight squeaks, and I've got out of them. I know the odds, but I have two friends who will back my play. I think we can handle Landon."

"It's not just Landon," the judge said sharply. "He's got some mean bastards on his payroll who will fight for him." He picked up his pipe and knocked the dottle from it. "Tell me something, Delaney. Why would any logical man . . . and you seem to be one . . . take on a job like this that common sense says you can't win?"

I was convinced by now that the judge could be trusted, so I said: "It isn't always common sense that makes us do a lot of the things we do. I haven't known Kate very long, but I don't need to. I love her. I have every right to think she loves me."

"I was beginning to wonder if that was the case," the judge said. "Or is it a matter of her being worth more than one hundred thousand dollars when, and if, she lives to collect it?"

I felt a quick thrust of anger boil up in me, but I realized it was a natural question, and I sensed that Bailey thought a great deal of Kate. He had a right to ask it.

"You can think what you damned please," I said. "I'm riding to the Diamond M as soon as I leave Rolly. I want to get a look at Landon."

He didn't show the surprise I thought he would. He said: "I take back what I said about you being a logical man. That would be the most insane thing for you to do that I can think of."

"Then I'm insane," I said. "A man can't always play the

right odds. I have to take chances, Judge."

He shrugged his shoulders as if to say it was too stupid to discuss. He said: "And after that, if you live long enough to ride away from the Diamond M?"

"I aim to bring Kate here, so you can read the will," I said. "I'm going to sit right here in this office and listen to it no matter what Landon says or thinks."

A tight grin touched the old man's face. "You think you and your friends can protect Kate long enough to get the will read?"

"We can do it," I said.

"When?"

"Day after tomorrow," I said. "You name the time."

"Three in the afternoon," he said.

"Fine." I nodded. "I'll have her here."

"I'll see that Landon is notified," he said.

I rose, and said: "Judge, this situation would have been more or less normal twenty years ago, with the law being what it was in a mining camp, but I just don't savvy how it could be happening now."

"Who do we turn to?" he demanded. "I can preside over a trial, but I can't make a jury come to a just decision, not as long as the jurors know what will happen to them if they decide against Landon. I can't go out to the Diamond M and force Landon off the premises. I can't protect Kate from a murderer's bullet. Can you?"

"I can," I said, "and I will."

I turned and left the judge's office.

# Chapter Fourteen

I had accomplished one of the things I had set out to do—make a date for the reading of Red Muldoon's will. The next step was to get Kate here for that reading, but that would have to wait a couple of days. I had also made my estimate of Judge Bailey. He was honest, and he would do what he could for Kate, but he was close to being helpless. I guess I had known that all the time. Justice, of course, could not exist where there was no enforcement of the law.

I had no idea that anyone else I talked to in Rolly would add to that impression, but it was too late to ride to the Diamond M that day. I had my room in the hotel, so I might just as well use it. I decided to feel the pulse of the town as completely as I could. If there was any help to be had, I'd find it.

My next step was the bank. I found it to be just about what I expected, a large room with four tellers' cages, a number of desks behind the cages where bookkeepers could work. Behind the desks were five doors marked **Private**. I supposed they were offices where the bank officials had transacted business in the glory days, but the bank, as with the rest of the town, was no more than a shell of what it had been.

Now only one man sat at a desk, and, as far as I could see, there was no one else in the bank. He rose and moved to one of the tellers' cages, asking: "What can I do for you?"

He was an old man, not as old as Judge Bailey, but old by my reckoning. He was big and running to fat with a large, untrimmed white beard that reminded me of a child's bib tied around his neck and pulled up tight under his chin.

I'd always had a notion that bankers were tight-fisted, miserly men who were utterly lacking in human kindness. Not that I'd ever had any experience with them. It was just a mental image I had, but it didn't fit this man. I had a crazy feeling that this man—I remembered Kate saying his name was Adam Jessup—was a personification of Santa Claus.

"My name is Del Delaney," I said. "I'd like to talk to you, if you have the time. I represent Kate Muldoon."

His expression changed instantly. He drew back, suddenly suspicious as he eyed me much as a wild animal might when he is suddenly alerted to possible danger. His eyes narrowed, his whole body tensed, then after a moment he said: "I have the time."

He opened the gate at the end of the counter and motioned for me to sit across from him as he dropped into the swivel chair he had been occupying before I came in.

"Is Kate alive and well?" he asked.

"Yes, but not due to Max Landon's efforts," I said bluntly. "He has sent three men to kill her. Two of them are dead. One told me Landon had hired him to murder her."

He was not a strong man, I thought, certainly not possessing the inner strength that Judge Bailey had. I sensed that he was honestly relieved that Kate was alive, but at the same time he was so frightened that it was hard for him to keep his composure.

Jessup folded his hands across his round belly, stared warily at me for a moment, than asked: "Where is she?"

"I can't tell you that," I said, "but I will see that she is in Rolly day after tomorrow to hear her father's will read. Judge Bailey has promised to notify Landon. Of course, all of that does not concern you personally, but I thought. . . ."

"Oh, yes it does concern me personally," he interrupted, lifting his gaze to meet mine. "Everybody in town is on Kate's side in this matter, so it concerns all of us. The trouble is we don't know how to meet the problem."

"The problem being Max Landon," I said.

He nodded. "That's right. The law is of no help. Perhaps you are aware of the situation?"

"I sure as hell am," I said, "and I'm making it my business to see that Kate gets a fair deal. As I understand it, Landon has possession of the Muldoon spread. Of course, nobody except the judge knows what the will says, but by rights the outfit should go to Kate. If the will leaves all of the estate to Landon, there isn't much Kate can do but sue to break the will. On the other hand, if the will leaves the property to Kate, and if Landon refuses to give up possession of the ranch, which he probably will, there is something we can do. I've been told that the estate, cash and ranch, would add up to more than a hundred thousand dollars. Is that correct?"

"That, my friend," he said irritably, "is none of your business. You should know that I can't divulge the bank's business or the business of the depositors to a stranger."

"It *is* my business," I said, my tone as sharp as his. "Kate has hired me and two of my friends who will back my play. If the law doesn't operate in this county, then we'll take the law into our own hands. She has hired us as bodyguards for one hundred dollars a day, and that piles up into pretty big money. I have a right to know if her father's estate can pay her obligations. As far as I'm concerned, I'd work for Kate for nothing, but I can't ask my friends to do that."

He was still a badly frightened man. I wasn't sure why, unless he thought I was in cahoots with Landon and would repeat everything he said. Now he almost smiled and said:

"I can assure you that the estate can pay any reasonable amount of money that Kate needs for her protection. Red Muldoon was a wealthy man. As you said, none of us but Judge Bailey knows what the will says, and it may leave the bulk of his property to Landon."

"I don't savvy it," I said. "He must have been a smart man. Kate said he ran this county for years, but Landon has got to be a genuine stinker. Why couldn't Muldoon see it?"

Jessup shrugged his shoulders. "Since Red's death, Landon's had the whole country buffaloed. We're all afraid to lift a finger, but we are genuinely concerned about Kate."

"I still don't see how Landon could pull the wool over Red's eyes the way he did," I said, trying to find an answer that made sense.

"He simply was blind to anything Max did," Jessup said. "Red wanted a son, and Max filled the bill. It's that simple." He hesitated, then added: "I tried to tell Red once what Max was. He flew off the handle and said I was a liar and he ought to break my neck. I never tried again. It was the same with the judge."

I guess I understood, but it still didn't add up to any sense. I had known parents who never wanted to hear about the rotten things their kids did. Never knowing Muldoon, I couldn't make a judgment of him. He must have been smart, but blind to the facts. Max Landon was not his son, but obviously Muldoon in his old age must have thought of him as a son, so I guess he was about the same caliber as those people I had known who had thought their sons were paragons of virtue.

I rose, knowing there was nothing more he could tell me. Before I turned to leave, he said: "You look like a competent man, but being competent against a man like Landon is not enough, not with the hardcase crew he's hired. You and your friends would have to be giants or magicians with your guns."

"I'll admit I was hoping for some help," I said. "It doesn't strike me that Landon has any friends in town."

He shook his head. "It hurts my pride, and I guess that back in the days of our youth I wouldn't be saying this, but we don't have any fight left in us. You'll find no help in Rolly to fight Max Landon. We know him. We don't know you, and we're going to have to live with Max." He made an inclusive gesture, adding: "The bank is all I have. It's not much these days, but it's a living for me and my wife. If Landon withdraws the Diamond M's business, I'd be broke."

I looked at him, knowing then why he was as scared as he was. I was convinced that, if I talked to the storekeeper or the saloonman or any of the other businessmen in Rolly, I'd get the same response.

I strode to the door, angered and yet vaguely knowing that I might feel the same way if I had been the age of these men, and if I knew Max Landon as well as they did. It was the old situation that I think we all find ourselves in at times, of condemning someone else without ever having been in their boots.

Before I opened the door, he said: "I'd like to help. I guess all of us would. Call us cowards if you want to, Delaney. We've talked about it many times. We are not proud of ourselves, but we have to do what we think is best for us."

I paused long enough to look back at him, seeing a man who had aged ten years in the few minutes I had been with him. He was having a very honest look at himself, and he was ashamed. Suddenly I found myself feeling more compassion for him than I had ever thought I would.

"I don't call you anything, Mister Jessup," I said, and stepped outside into the bright sunshine.

# Chapter Fifteen

I walked to the end of the block and turned right, reached a side street, and followed it. All the time a question kept pounding at my mind. Was Kate's position here as hopeless as it seemed? She knew Max Landon very well. So did Judge Bailey and Adam Jessup. Was I a fool to pursue a course that seemed bound to end in disaster? I finally decided it boiled down to how much I wanted to live.

I could not dismiss the question as easily as I would have liked, and all the time I was very much aware that the problem was as old as time. I knew how Kate felt. She had told me more than once that all the money that was rightfully hers was not worth my life. I also knew that was no answer to me.

I came to a church, a log building set some distance back from the street, with a small cabin behind it that apparently was a parsonage. A man was working in a garden in the back of the churchyard. On impulse I walked around the church building to him.

The man didn't know I was there until I said: "Howdy."

Startled, he turned, then straightened up, and leaned on his hoe. "Well now," he said, grinning, "if this was Indian country, I'd have been scalped before I knew you were there." He held out a hand to me as he added: "I'm the Reverend Charles Nathrop, the shepherd of a small flock that meets here every Sunday morning."

"I'm Del Delaney," I said, and shook hands.

He was a tall, lanky man with a lantern jaw and prominent ears that looked as if they had been set to propel him forward each time the wind blew. I had never seen ears like his and wondered how much of a burden they had been to him back in his school days when kids gave nicknames to their schoolmates based on such peculiarities.

I liked him. It was one of those instinctive reactions to another man that I seldom had. Maybe it was because he was a homely man, or because he had a firm handshake, or maybe because I sensed a quality in him that set him apart from other men I had met in Rolly. Maybe, just maybe, I thought, he had lived with trouble and adversity long enough to know that a man can't measure life and property and the problems of life in the way the Rolly men did.

"You're a stranger to Rolly," he said. "I want to invite you to our services Sunday morning." He grinned again, and I was aware that he had the widest mouth I had ever seen on a man. "I'm not trying to convert you. It's just that it would be a good way to get acquainted, if you are going to live here." Then he made a kind of waving gesture with his right hand, the left still clutching the hoe handle. "I guess, as usual, I am assuming too much. Maybe you have no intention of living in Rolly."

"Not at the moment," I said. "Do you know Kate Muldoon?"

The good humor left his face. "Of course, I know Kate. She disappeared from her hotel room more than a week ago. Do you know anything about her?"

"She's alive and well," I told him. "I have arranged for her to be in town day after tomorrow to hear Judge Bailey read her father's will."

Relief flowed across his homely face and was almost immediately replaced by fear. He dropped his hoe handle and clutched both my arms. "I don't know who you are, Mister

Delaney, or what kind of motives would prompt you to do that, but I implore you not to bring her here. She'll be killed. Everyone in town was afraid she was killed when she disappeared from her hotel room."

"Max Landon has tried three times to get her killed," I said. "The night she disappeared I was the one who took her out of town. She's safe. She knows we've got to bring this business to a head. Maybe she will get killed. Maybe I will, but there's no other way to handle this problem. I will not stand still and see her lose her inheritance."

He dropped his hands to his side and stepped back. "What is your interest in her?"

I felt a charge of resentment churn through me just as I had before when someone had suggested I was interested in her inheritance, but again I kept a tight rein on my temper. It was a natural question, and I knew I had to expect it. I said: "She hired me and two of my friends to serve as body-guards. We'll be with her."

"Three men are not enough," he snapped. "I don't suppose you know Max Landon?"

"I've never met him," I answered, "but I intend to meet him tomorrow, if I can find him. Tell me something. How can one man tree a community the way he's treed Rolly?"

"Partly by threatening to ruin people's business which he has the power and money to do," Nathrop said, "or at least he will when he actually owns the Diamond M. The rest is the threat of physical danger. I've seen him beat up people just to show us how we stand. I saw him do it once on Main Street. I tried to interfere, but he knocked me down and kicked in my ribs. He broke three of them."

I was not surprised, and I wondered whether physical danger or his financial power were the greater force that had intimidated Rolly. I said: "People speak well of Red

Muldoon. No one speaks well of Max Landon. Why did Muldoon think so much of him and possibly leave the ranch to him? People have tried to explain this to me, but it never makes any sense."

"Kate has probably told you," he said, "and it never makes much sense to me. A man sees only what he wants to see. Red wanted Landon as the son he never had, a son who would run the Diamond M the way Red ran it."

That was little different from what I'd heard before, but I wanted to hear it from the preacher. At least, he was a man who had no business to lose if he bucked Landon.

"You tell me that three men are not enough," I said. "I was hoping to find some men in Rolly who would help me protect Kate when she gets here. I haven't found any yet."

He dragged a toe through the moist soil, staring at the ground for a time, then he turned to look squarely at me. He said: "The Lord sent His people to smite the Philistines. I can do no less. When the time comes, I'll help. Let me know when you need me, but I will help whether you call on me or not, if I know when it's time."

So far I had met the response in Rolly I had expected. I had seen it as almost a ghost town, a town that should have been blown away by the winds of progress long ago, a town of old men who had lost their courage and allowed themselves to be run over by a bully. I had not expected this response from a preacher.

I held out a hand. "By God, sir," I said, and added apologetically, "excuse the profanity. It just popped out before I could stop it. What I want to say is that I'm glad to find one man with guts in this worthless town. Maybe I'll find some more."

He shook my hand, pleased, I think. "I doubt that you will. Except for the sheriff, I'm the youngest man in town. It takes a certain amount of youth, either in age or spirit, to fight. The spirit just isn't here."

"What about the sheriff?" I asked.

"Go see him," he answered, scowling. "Then you can make your own judgment."

I left him then, not knowing whether he would deliver when the time came or not, but I was encouraged. I turned back into Main Street, and, as I approached the Miner's Bar, I saw a man push his way through the batwings and walk toward me. I stopped, hit by the feeling I had seen him before, then I knew. He was the one who had tried to smother Kate.

My first impulse was to draw my gun and kill the man just as I would kill a mad dog, but I didn't let my impulse get the best of me. He was weaving a little and singing in an off-key some tune about going back to Texas. He didn't see me, and I doubt that he would have recognized me if he had looked at me, as surprised and shocked as he had been the night I yanked him off Kate's bed and hit him.

I waited until he was two steps past me, then I drew my gun and rammed it into his back as I said: "You make a move for your iron and you're dead."

He stopped and put his hands up, breathing hard. He said: "I ain't got no *dinero* on me."

"Keep moving," I said. "Turn left up the hill to the courthouse. We're going to have a visit with the sheriff. Put your hands down."

He obeyed, mumbling, but making no resistance, and we made the turn at the end of the block. He was breathing hard, and, by the time we had climbed to the bench where the courthouse stood, he was panting. He paused at the front of the steps to ask: "You got some charge against me?"

"Attempted murder will do for a start," I said. "Keep moving."

He climbed the steps to the first floor before he fully understood what I'd said. He stopped and turned his head to stare at me, asking: "Who do you think I tried to murder?"

"Kate Muldoon."

I thought his eyes were going to pop out of his head. He'd been laboring for breath, but now he didn't even try to take a breath for several seconds. He just stood there, slack-jawed and staring at me, then he sucked in a long breath and said accusingly: "So you're the hairpin who beat hell out of me that night."

I could see a door at the far end of the hall that held faded letters announcing **Sheriff**. "Straight ahead," I said, nudging him with the muzzle of my gun.

He moved on along the hall, cursing. Before he reached the sheriff's office, he said: "You know Max Landon will kill you for this, don't you?"

"So he's the one who paid you to murder Kate," I said, as if I hadn't known all the time. "Kate wondered who wanted her dead bad enough to pay an idiot like you to botch the job."

He didn't say anything more as we walked through the door into the sheriff's office. A fat man was sitting at a desk reading a newspaper. He looked up, nodded at my prisoner, and said: "You got into some trouble, Bill?"

"It's a damned lie," the man shouted. "I never seen this jasper before in my life, and he's got a cock 'n' bull story about me trying to kill some woman named Kate Muldoon. I don't know no Kate Muldoon."

The sheriff leaned back, his chair creaking as he shifted his weight. He eyed me as he took a half-smoked cigar from an ashtray and put it into his mouth. He lit it, stared at me through the smoke for another half minute, then asked: "What's your name, stranger?"

"Del Delaney," I said. "In case you're interested, Kate Muldoon is alive and well."

If he was surprised, he didn't show it. He said: "Put your gun up, Delaney, and sit down. You can go, Bill. I have no proof that what this man said is true, and I don't know who the hell he is. Chances are he's got it in for you and wants to make trouble. I've seen his kind before."

I sat down and stared blankly at Sheriff Windy Holt. I couldn't believe what I'd just heard.

# Chapter Sixteen

The man I'd brought in tore out of Holt's office as if his tail was on fire. I kept staring at the mass of blubber who called himself a sheriff and made up my mind about him just as the preacher had told me to do. He was no threat to Max Landon.

I judged that Holt was about my age, maybe six feet tall, with fat bulging from all parts of his body. I doubt that he could have ridden a horse half a mile. The only reason he could have been elected sheriff was that nobody else wanted the job. In a county as small as this one, there would be no deputies, and the pay must be a piddling figure.

Holt shifted the cigar in his mouth, scooted his chair up close to his desk, and opened a drawer. He took out a stack of papers that appeared to be reward dodgers and began thumbing through them. I got up, knowing there wasn't a thing I could do about jailing the man who had tried to kill Kate, when Holt snarled: "Get back into that chair! I'll tell you when you can leave."

Sitting down, I realized I had made a mistake giving my real name, but I was tired of telling people I was Del Del when I had to give a last name. I simply had not believed that a phony charge like the one against me would be known this far from Montana. There were too many horse thieves, murderers, and bank robbers for a law man to worry about a rape charge that might have been committed a thousand miles away.

"You've got nothing against me," I said, and got up again.

"Damn it, sit down and stay down till I tell you to get up!" Holt bellowed.

He was hunched over his desk, one hand working through the stack of papers, the other hidden from my sight. I was sure he was holding a gun on me, and, if I made a wrong move, he'd drill me in a second. If he killed me, claiming I was resisting arrest, nothing would be done to him, but I'd be dead. So I sat down again, and for the first time it hit me that I was in trouble. Holt knew or suspected that the man I'd brought in was on Landon's payroll, and the last thing he wanted to do was to cross Landon.

"Your name sounds familiar," Holt said. "Your face looks familiar, too, but right now I can't place it. You're a wanted man somewhere. I know you are."

Sid Blackwell, sitting up there in Prairie City, had done a good job circulating the fact that I was wanted. He couldn't have done any better if I'd knocked the bank over. Now all I could do was to sit here and wait for Holt to throw me into jail. I knew he was going to, whether he found the right reward dodger or not.

Holt kept working through the papers as he watched me, hoping I'd make a move. When I didn't, he urged me, saying: "Go ahead. Head for the door. I'll kill you, and it will be in line of duty, shooting a man who was fleeing from the law."

"And you'd get a little something from Max Landon to pay you for your trouble," I said.

"I'm a good law man," he said smugly, "and Mister Landon rewards a man for doing his duty."

"I'll bet he does," I said hotly. "He hired three men to murder the girl who stands between him and Red Muldoon's fortune, but you wouldn't touch him, would you?"

"Your accusation is ridiculous, and I'll pretend you didn't say it," he said, "being new in town and all. Mister Landon is a decent, law-abiding pillar in the community. Nobody talks about him the way you did just now."

"You must be stone deaf if you haven't heard anyone talk that way," I said. "I haven't been in the county very long, and I've heard worse talk than that."

He shrugged his fat shoulders. "You can always find somebody who doesn't like somebody else."

He picked up a reward dodger, studied it, and nodded. "Here we are. Wanted in Prairie City, Montana, for rape. This here drawing looks like you." He tipped his head back, a smug expression on his face. "Well, now, I consider rape the lowest crime in the book. We'll just hold you on ice. Take your gun belt off, slow-like, and drop it on the floor beside your chair, then get up and mosey over yonder to that cell."

He rose and, as I had guessed, held a gun in his right hand. I thought about making a run for it, or pulling my gun, or trying to get close enough to slam my fist into his gut. All were suicidal ideas, with him holding a gun on me the way he was. So I unlatched my gun belt and dropped it to the floor, then walked into the cell he had indicated. He slammed the door shut, stood leering at me as if he had me exactly where he wanted me, and I guess he did.

"I'll go over to the telegraph office and wire Prairie City that you turned up here and for them to come and get you. Chances are you raped the banker's daughter and there's a reward out for you."

Sid Blackwell could come and get me, all right, and take me back to Prairie City, laughing every step of the way. I'd have a hell of a trip back with him, and the chances were Sid would find some excuse to shoot me before we got to Montana.

135

Holt was waddling toward the door when I yelled at him: "Tell Judge Bailey what you've done with me."

He wheeled, startled, I guess, because I had mentioned Judge Bailey. Then he was angry. "Well, by God, so you think that old fool is on your side, do you?" he shouted. "Let me tell you something, friend. He don't do a very good job handling his end of things, and he don't have nothing to do with the way I run the sheriff's office, so forget him."

This time, when he turned toward the door, he kept moving. I sat down on my filthy bunk and told myself I was in a hell of a fix. I couldn't break out. I didn't have any friends who could help. Smith and the Kid wouldn't even know I was in jail. If Landon got word about me from the fellow who had tried to murder Kate, he'd find a way to kill me right here in this cell.

It wasn't so much, though, that I worried about being killed while I was in jail, at least not for more than a minute or two. It was just the fact that I had lost my freedom. The stink was sickening, a combination, I thought, of stale sweat and urine and vomit. I had never been in a jail before, but I supposed they all smelled this way, at least in small counties that didn't have money to hire a janitor. If it was left up to Windy Holt, and I assumed it was, the place would rot and fall down on his head before he'd turn a hand toward cleaning it up.

Still, I could stand the stink. What really was the burr under my saddle was the fact that I was locked up in this tiny cell that wasn't any bigger than my mother's pantry back in Prairie City. I sat there on the bunk, my nerves growing tighter by the minute, and thought about what had happened to put me here.

Sure, I could cuss myself about coming here and giving Holt my real name, but, when I tried to be logical, I told myself I had every right to believe that no one in Prairie City would be vindictive enough to mail reward dodgers to sheriffs a thousand miles away and across the width of almost three states. Or that out of hundreds of reward dodgers that Holt would receive in a year, he'd be the kind of man who could remember the name of a man wanted in a distant state and for a crime that most sheriffs would consider a minor offense. Horse stealing would have been a different matter.

I finally got so wound up that I rose and paced back and forth, but the space was too small to do much pacing. I could take three steps one way, and then I had to turn around and go back the other way. I had never been penned up anywhere before, but I had known what it would do to me. I simply couldn't stand being locked up. That was why I had run, but it hadn't done any good. Here I was, locked up in Windy Holt's stinking jail.

I sat down on the cot again, feeling as if I had some tiny, savage animals clawing through my body. I wanted to get up and beat my fists against the bars, or batter my head against the wall, but I didn't panic that much. I knew damned well, though, that if I was stuck here very long that was exactly what I'd be doing. Then I thought of Kate.

I wished I could have forgotten Kate and kept my mind on my own troubles. If I didn't get out of here, and it sure as hell didn't look as if I would, I'd never ride out to the Diamond M tomorrow as I'd planned, and Kate wouldn't be here for the reading of the will as I had promised Judge Bailey.

If Kate wasn't here, I wondered if Landon would get the Diamond M by default. Not likely, I thought, but the situation couldn't go on being up in the air forever. One thing I did know was that Judge Bailey would consider me less than dependable, and it wouldn't help me with Kate, either, and that was more important than how Bailey felt about me.

I sat there trembling and sweating, my thoughts jumping from one crazy notion to another. I knew none of them would work, but I also knew I couldn't stay here. If I was still in jail when Sid Blackwell showed up, I'd be on my way back to Montana before I knew it. Smith and the Kid would break me out of here if they knew where I was, but I had no way of letting either one know.

It seemed to me I sat there for hours thinking about the fix I was in. Nobody brought me any supper, but then I wasn't hungry. I hadn't thought about food until I noticed through the small cell window that the sun was almost down. Just as I became aware of that, Windy Holt stomped into his office.

The minute Holt slammed the door, I knew something had gone wrong with his plans. He took a key off the wall, unlocked my cell door, and said: "Vamoose. Get out."

I had never heard sweeter words in my life. I didn't waste any time obeying him. I picked up my gun belt from the desk where Holt had dropped it and buckled it around me as I walked toward the door. I turned and stared at Holt, and thought I had never seen a more sour look on a man's face in my life than I saw on his. He'd been so sure he had me dead to rights and probably would have a reward coming that whatever information had come in over the wire must have been very bad news.

I had a right to know what he'd heard, and, now that I had my gun, I was damned sure he wasn't locking me up again. I asked: "What'd you hear from Prairie City?"

"The rape charge has been dropped," he said, glowering at me as if I had been guilty of some wrong-doing. "The woman who brought the charge against you left town. Now get to hell out of here before I change my mind. I want you out of town first thing in the morning."

I didn't leave as fast as he told me. I stood there, staring at him and feeling as if I owned the earth. It wasn't just that I felt good about being free again and the rape charge dropped. I had a heady sense of triumph, and I had no intention right then of doing anything he told me to do. "I read something about the best-laid plans of mice and men," I said, grinning as I looked at him.

"I don't know what the hell you're talking about," he growled. "Just get out of here or I'll throw you back into that cell again."

"I didn't think you'd know what I was talking about," I said. "I'll tell you something else. You'll never throw me back into that stinking cell."

I walked out then. When I was outside, I just stood motionless for a time, breathing in the sweet-smelling air. Then I suddenly realized I was hungry and headed for the hotel.

## Chapter Seventeen

When I reached the hotel, I climbed the stairs to my room and washed the best I could in the tepid water that was in the pitcher. I wondered if I'd ever get the stench of that cell off my body. As I dried my face and hands, I could still smell it.

I went downstairs to the dining room, hoping to get there before they closed. I did, but only by a few minutes. I started to sit down at the first table I saw, then noticed that Judge Bailey was sitting by himself near a street window, so I crossed the dining room to him.

He looked up, saw who I was, and nodded at the chair across the table from him. "Sit down," he said. "I was just lingering here hoping you'd show up. The waitress said no stranger had been in for supper, but I thought you had to come in sooner or later, seeing as this is the only decent place to eat in town."

"I'm not sure you want me to sit down at the same table with you," I said. "Smell anything?"

He shook his head negatively. "Why?"

"I've been a guest in Windy Holt's hotel for a few hours," I answered. "The cell stunk worse'n any place I'd ever been in. I thought I might be carrying it with me."

"Now what in hell did Windy have against you?" he demanded.

I sat down and told him what had happened. He listened, then shook his head in disgust. "He was working for a reward, all right," Bailey said. "That would be like him, though why a county as far away as yours would put up

140

money for a fugitive on a rape charge is beyond me."

"Maybe it was more'n the hope of getting a reward," I said. "Suppose he knew the fellow I brought in worked for Landon. He'd figure that turning him loose and holding me would give him a boost with Landon."

He nodded. "You're probably right. He goes with the wind. He used to be all for Red Muldoon, and now he's for Landon, figuring that whoever runs the Diamond M runs the county. He's not far off the truth, either."

The waitress came and took my order. The judge said: "Give me a little more of that tar you call coffee, Martha."

She acted insulted, then winked at me. "It ain't that bad, Judge, and you know it."

"All I know is that it's been corroding the lining of my stomach for years," he said.

She sniffed. "As much coffee as you drink would corrode anybody's stomach," she said, and made a great pretense of huffing back to the kitchen.

The judge spooned sugar into his coffee. "It's a funny thing, Delaney. When I was a kid in Ohio, we had a field of cabbage in front of the house. One winter we got a hell of an early freeze that froze the cabbage. It rotted right there in the field, and you can't imagine the stink it made. I smelled it anywhere I went and thought it was on me and that I couldn't get rid of it. It wasn't, of course, so I guess a smell like that just gets lodged in your nose and you smell it even when it's not there."

"Holt ought to clean up his jail," I said, "or have the janitor do it. It's not right to make a prisoner suffer that way."

"It makes for unusual and cruel punishment," the judge admitted, "but it's a poor county, and we don't have the tax money to even pay the county officials, so we don't have a janitor for the courthouse. Everybody cleans up his own office, but, hell, Windy wouldn't pull his boots on if he didn't get sore feet walking barefoot."

My soup came, and I started to eat, then looked up. "He didn't even bring me any supper."

"He doesn't feed anybody unless he keeps them for more'n a day," the judge said. "He bills the county, and, if the county gets around to paying the bill, he sticks the money in his pocket, and the hotel hollers for its pay. If it hollers long enough, he'll eventually pay." He kept stirring his coffee, staring at me thoughtfully. "There was a time when we had plenty of tax money and we paid our officials. We had two janitors for the courthouse. Now the mines don't pay taxes, and we just don't have enough to go around. Sometimes I have to wait three months for my salary."

"You've got some ranches," I said. "Don't you get any taxes out of them?"

He nodded. "Some. Trouble is, they're all small outfits except the Diamond M. Red always said he kept the county going, but it takes more than he paid to keep us even. There's a little town property here in Rolly, but business is so bad that some folks don't pay their taxes." He glanced up at me. "I like to think of the old days when this was a boom camp and there was something going on all the time. Red was never sheriff, but he always backed the sheriff until his health got so bad he couldn't leave the house. If the sheriff didn't do his job, Red was after him, and he got busy in a hurry." Bailey spread his hands in a gesture of despair. "I just don't know, Delaney. I'm the judge. Looks like I could do something, but I can't do a damned thing if the sheriff doesn't enforce my rulings or collect the fines I levy on folks."

I thought about it as I ate. After a few minutes of silence,

I said: "Where does this leave Kate?"

"That's what's worrying me," Bailey said, "and, believe me, I've done a lot of worrying ever since Red died. Not only because I like Kate and want her to get what's hers, but because the Diamond M is so important to the politics and economy of the county. Even with you working for Kate, I can't see how she's going to get a fair shake, regardless of the will. I don't think you can handle Landon even with a couple of good men to back you up."

I finished my meal and leaned back, a coffee cup in my hand. "The truth is, Judge, I don't know if I can or not. I guess I just don't know how good a man I am. I don't think any man does until he's been tried."

He seemed to be measuring me, his gaze pinned on my face. He was, I thought, a pathetic old man who lived in the past and had no idea how to solve today's problems. Nobody else did, either, except Max Landon. He knew what he wanted and how far he would go to get it, so it was up to me, and that, I thought, was a hell of a fix for a man to be in.

"Max will keep trying," Bailey said somberly as he rose. "Well, I've got to get home, but I'll buy you a drink before I go."

"That's an offer I can't turn down," I said as I rose.

I paused at the desk to pay for my meal, crossed the lobby, and followed the judge into the bar. It was almost empty, just a couple of cowboys drinking at a table, and one man facing the bartender across the mahogany.

The man's back was to me, and it wasn't until I reached the bar that I had a look at his face and recognized him. I guess I said something aloud. I don't have any idea what it was, but the words were jolted out of me when I saw he was the man who had attempted to murder Kate and I'd tried to get arrested earlier in the day.

He swung around to look at me, then he started to back away, his face turning ghastly white. He wheeled and began to run, but, before he reached the back door, he wheeled and yelled—"You ain't gonna shoot me in the back!"—and went for his gun.

I hadn't expected that. I thought he was high-tailing it out of the bar, so I was a little slow getting my gun clear of leather. He had one clean shot at me before I could squeeze the trigger, and, if he hadn't been so scared he was trembling, I would have been a dead man. But he was jumpy, he hurried his shot, and he missed.

The man's shot came nearer to hitting the judge than it did me. In any case, I fixed it so he didn't get another chance. I nailed him squarely in the brisket. The force of the slug slammed him against the wall, his gun hand relaxing, his Colt dropping to the floor. He hung there a few seconds, his head drooping, then began to sag. His feet slid out from under him, and he sprawled on the floor.

There was a moment of silence, the echoes of the two shots hammering at my ears as they slowly died, amplified, I suppose, by the confines of the narrow room. Gunsmoke writhed and twisted as it slowly rose into the still air gradually to disappear. The cowboys were on their feet, startled by what had happened, their eyes on the fallen man.

"I think maybe you'll do, Delaney," the judge said. "Damned if I don't." He jerked a thumb at one of the cowboys. "Curly, go fetch Windy Holt. He's usually playing cards in the Red Slipper this time of night."

The cowboy nodded and ran out of the bar. The judge paced slowly toward the man, knelt beside him, and felt for his pulse, then rose. "You didn't take any chances with that shot. He's as dead as a mackerel. Who is he?"

"Called himself Clay Morgan," the bartender said. "Been hanging around here two, three weeks. Never said where he came from, or where he was going, or what he wanted. Funny thing, though. He always had money."

The judge turned to me. "I never saw a man scare another man by just looking at him the way you scared this *hombre*. What did it?"

"He knew I'd kill him, or beat hell out of him which might have been worse." I had holstered my gun and leaned against the bar, a little uneasy now that it was over, and sick, too. Self-defense or not, I knew I would never get used to killing a man. "I guess I didn't tell you, Judge. He was the hairpin who tried to murder Kate in her hotel room."

"The hell." Bailey stared at me as if he couldn't believe it. "He's the man you tried to get Windy to jail."

I nodded. "That's right."

"Then he wasn't just scared of what you'd do to him," the judge said thoughtfully. "He was afraid you'd spread the word, and he knew he'd be in trouble when folks heard."

Holt came in, took a look at me, lips curling in distaste as he said: "So it's you again. You just can't stay out of trouble, can you?" He walked to where the dead man lay, stooped to feel for his pulse, then straightened up, and swung around to face me. "Lay your gun on the table, mister. This time you're staying in jail."

I dropped my hand to the butt of my gun. "Try putting me there, fat man," I said.

"My God, Windy!" the judge exploded. "I knew you were stupid, but I didn't believe even you could be this stupid. You'd better ask a few questions before you try to arrest anybody."

Holt got red in the face. "I ain't got no strangle hold on stupidity, Judge. He beefed this jasper, didn't he? That's all

I need to know. He's a troublemaker and will be until I get him back into jail."

"You've never seen trouble before like what you're going to see if you try throwing me back into your stinking jail," I said.

I still had my hand on the butt of my gun, and I'd have killed Holt if he'd gone ahead with his try at arresting me. Bucking sheriffs was getting to be a habit, and, when I thought about the hours I'd spent in Holt's jail, I'd have done anything I needed to do to stay out of it.

"Then I'll get a posse together and we'll string you up right now," Holt threatened.

"Oh, no, you won't," the judge said. "You might start asking what started the fight and why Delaney shot him. There is such a thing as self-defense."

"You mean Morgan drew first?" Holt asked as if that was incredible.

"He sure did," the judge said. "You expect Delaney to stand here and let himself be killed without defending himself?"

"I ain't real sure I believe you, Judge," Holt said. "What about it, Mack?"

The barkeep nodded. "The judge called it right, Windy. This man didn't have any choice, if he wanted to live."

Holt turned to the two cowboys, who nodded agreement. Holt said reluctantly: "All right, Delaney, it was self-defense, but don't forget what I told you. Be out of town before noon tomorrow or you go back into the jug."

"What charge?" I asked.

He shrugged. "Vagrancy will do. No visible means of support." He motioned to the cowboys. "Get Mack's door out of the back room and tote Morgan's carcass over to the undertaker's."

He walked toward the door, moving swiftly and not looking back. The judge said: "If you ever come up in my court, Windy, I'll remember you called me a liar tonight."

Holt went on out of the bar and into the street, still not looking at us or saying a word. Maybe he thought I might shoot him in the back, and I'll admit the thought crossed my mind. I had a hunch he was either going to flip-flop in his support of Landon, or I would shoot him before this was over. I could not think of any man I'd ever met that I held in more contempt than I did Windy Holt.

"Let's have that drink, Delaney," the judge said. "Windy's not very bright, but he's got a notion about you and Landon. I'd bet on it."

Holt wasn't very bright if he hadn't figured out how I felt about Landon. What had happened seemed to me to prove that Holt was Landon's man, or, at least, he was at the moment. Of course, he'd change sides if it was to his advantage, but he might find it very difficult to go on carrying the star if Landon was out of the picture.

The bartender poured our drinks as the judge said: "You're still going to the Diamond M tomorrow?"

"That's right," I said.

"Then you are a damned fool," he said in disgust. "You'll never get off that spread alive."

"I will if I don't run into his whole crew," I said.

"We need you here," Bailey said angrily. "My God, man, where do I stand if you get yourself beefed?"

"Sorry, Judge," I said. "It's a chance I've got to take. The trick is to avoid Landon's crew."

That, I knew, depended strictly on luck.

## Chapter Eighteen

I woke at dawn the next morning and lay in bed for a few minutes, thinking of the day ahead and trying to work out in my mind what I would do in the different situations I might face. I'm not usually a praying man. In fact, I seldom even thought about praying, but Judge Bailey's words kept ringing in my ears: *You'll never get off that spread alive.* So before I got out of bed, I did a little praying. If Providence had a hand in my looking after Kate Muldoon, today was the day that would test how much help I was getting.

I shaved, dressed, and went downstairs for breakfast. I paid my hotel bill and stepped out into the almost cold mountain air; I looked up and down the street, deserted at this early hour, and wondered if I'd ever see it again. I told myself nothing would really be settled until the will was read, and maybe not even then. In any case, I had to get Kate here for that.

The sun was a full, red ball above the cañon rim to the east when I rode out of town. The judge had given me directions about getting to the Diamond M and how much riding time it would take. It added up to a long day before I'd get back to Kate and John Smith, so I didn't waste time, but took a steady pace down the cañon, past the turn-off to Aunt Becky's place, and on south along the river until the cañon widened into a fair-size valley, and the slopes on both sides of me began to flatten out, the craggy rims bright red in the morning light, color that made this valley one of the most beautiful places I had ever seen.

It was near noon when I came out of the valley and into the desert to the south with its sage brush and rabbit brush and junipers replacing the aspens and pines and spruce through which I had been riding. The river made a wide bend to the west here, and I could see the Diamond M buildings ahead of me on a bench above the stream. I rode directly to it, leaving the road and cutting across an alfalfa field, then climbing to the bench.

I dismounted in front of the house and tied to the hitch pole. For a time I stood motionless as I studied the place. The house was bigger than most ranch houses I had seen, a two-story frame structure with one-story additions on both ends. It struck me that Red Muldoon had added the wings after he had become wealthy so it would represent a man of power and affluence, but it had become seedy with time.

The doors and window frames needed painting, some shakes on the roof should be replaced, and the barbed-wire fence surrounding the house, woodshed, and privy was down in two places. The gate in front was held up by only one hinge, and it hung comically askew as I didn't have to open it, but simply stepped between the dangling gate and the juniper post to which it would normally have been hung.

As I walked up the path that led to the front door, I saw a few roses next to the wall of the house. They were trying to bloom, but the ground was so dry the bushes were withering. Obviously none of them had been watered for a long time. I was not used to seeing ranch houses with spacious lawns and well-cared for flowers, but it struck me that there had been a time when this yard had been carefully tended, probably by Kate, but now had received no attention whatever, so the whole place had a dilapidated appearance.

I knocked on the front door, but no one answered. Then

I pounded on it, but still no one came, so I turned and walked back to my horse. I stood motionless as I looked around at the corrals and the big barn and other outbuildings. A dozen or so horses were in a corral beside the barn, and a column of smoke was rising from the building that I guessed was the cook shack. Beyond that I saw no trace of life anywhere around the place, not even a dog.

Obviously Max Landon was not around, and that was disappointing. Judging from the position of the sun, it was noon. Landon was probably out with his crew. I walked slowly toward the cook shack, wondering if they would come riding in any moment, but I saw no hint of movement on the desert that ran for miles to the south and west.

The cook shack door was open, for the day had turned hot. When I reached the door, I stopped, looking inside at the cook who was wearing a white apron and was rolling out some pie dough on his work table. From the fragrant smell that flowed to me, I guessed he had more pies in the oven.

"Howdy," I said.

Startled, he looked up, scowled when he saw I was a stranger, and said roughly: "I ain't got no grub to put out for saddle bums who are riding through, so fork your horse and slope out of here."

He had a white, drooping mustache stained by tobacco juice. His hair was white, too, and from the wrinkled skin of his face I judged he was seventy or older. If he was Bill Rogers, and I was certain he was, he had come here when Red Muldoon had driven his first herd across the divide and started the Diamond M. Muldoon, if he had lived, would have been about the same age, I thought.

"You Bill Rogers?" I asked.

He hesitated, staring at me, the rolling pin gripped on both ends. "Won't do you no good to try to tell me we knew

150

each other at some time or other, or your daddy knew me when me 'n' Red was on the Pecos. Now git."

"I thought you'd like to know about Kate," I said. "She told me you were probably the only friend she had left on the ranch."

He released his grip on the rolling pin and straightened up, interest showing in his weathered face. "What do you know about Kate?" he demanded.

"Quite a bit," I said. "You knew she had got to Rolly?"

He wiped his hands on his apron and walked around the table to where I stood just inside the door. "Yeah, I knew that, and I likewise knew she disappeared from her hotel room. Now if you're bulling me, I'll take my sharpest butcher knife and open up your gizzard."

"I've got an idea you would," I said. "You'd better save your butcher knife for Landon. He tried three times to have her killed."

He swore, staring hard at me as if still not quite sure I was telling the truth, then he backed up to the table and sat down. "I ain't surprised," he said. "Max sure wants this layout, and he'd kill anybody to get it. He'll even look you in the eye and claim he's got it coming." He wiped a hand across his face. "But to murder Kate." He stopped. I guess he considered the idea too appalling even to think about. Finally he added: "Come on in and tell me about it. I'll get you a cup of coffee."

I stepped into the room and sat down across the table from where he had been working. Going to the stove, he returned with a cup and coffee pot and poured a cup for me. I talked as he worked, telling him what had happened, even to killing the man last night in Rolly.

"You sound like you're telling the truth," he said. "Knowing Max, I can believe it. He wanted Kate to marry

151

him, you know, but she saw through him better'n Red ever did. She wouldn't have anything to do with him. He's got a lot of pride, Max has, and I reckon he's never forgiven her. He'd probably like to see her dead on that account even if it wasn't for the spread. He's a mean bastard, but old Red, he was just too stubborn to see it in Max. He never seen anything that didn't jibe with what he thought the truth was." He drummed his fingertips on the table as he stared at me. "What'd you come out here for?"

"Don't tell me I'm an idiot," I said. "Judge Bailey has already told me, but I figured I might have a chance to catch Landon alone. I want him to know that Kate's alive and will be in town for the reading of the will tomorrow. If he flies off the handle and pulls his gun, maybe I'll be lucky enough to kill him. Seems to me that Kate will never get what's coming to her as long as Max Landon is alive."

"You ain't far off on that," Rogers said moodily.

"What about the crew?" I asked.

"They're his men," the cook said. "He's been bringing men in for the last six months. Red didn't know what was going on. Kate was dead right about me being the only friend she has left. I'm so old Max figured I was harmless, so he's kept me on."

Rogers kept staring at me as I sipped my coffee, still trying to measure me, I guess, to decide how well I'd stack up against Landon. I asked: "How can Landon be as powerful as he seems to be in this county?"

"Right now he represents the Diamond M," Rogers answered. "Maybe it's the reputation that Red gave the ranch when he was alive. Then he's smart. He knows how to manage people, who to threaten, and who to pat on the back." He leaned back as he thought about it, then he went on: "I've thought about this same question ever since Red got laid up, and Max started running the outfit. Maybe the point is Max don't have no conscience. At least, I never seen a trace of any. He'll lie while he's looking you right in the face, and you'll believe him. He'll take advantage of any weakness you've got. If you get in his way, he just plows you under. I don't know what in hell you think you can do to stop him."

"Even if the will leaves everything to Kate?"

He nodded. "You've seen the sheriff. What other way is there to enforce the law except through the sheriff's office? Max won't leave the Diamond M no matter whether the spread is his or not."

I could feel my stomach kicking up, and I wondered if there was any chance of getting the old man to cook a quick meal for me, but, before I could ask, he got up and walked to the door and stood there, staring out across the flat.

"You say Kate hired you as bodyguard," he said, "but you're doing a hell of a lot more'n that. I'm wondering if you're stuck on her."

I hesitated, thinking it was none of his business, but on the other hand he was Kate's friend, and he might be an important ally. I thought I could trust him, so I said: "I am. That's why I'm trying to see this through for her. I'm not asking for any favors. If she doesn't want me around when it's over, I won't be staying."

"She's a good girl," Rogers said, "and she's loyal as hell. Chances are, she's stuck on you, too. Her dad never let her go with boys, thinking they were all after her money, so she's never in her life had a man she could fall in love with. If you ever tell her I told you this, I'll skin you alive and hang your hide up to dry. Savvy?"

"You're a tough old bird," I said, "and I believe you."

He laughed. "I'm the biggest bluffer on this side of the

Mississippi, but, damn it, I'd do anything for Kate. She never did flirt with Max or encourage him, so what happened wasn't her fault. Like I said, Max asked Kate to marry him. Fact is, he asked her more'n once, but she always turned him down cold. When Red began showing he wasn't gonna live more'n a year or so, Max got too anxious. Last summer, when she was getting ready to go back to school, she went riding one afternoon, and Max followed her. He cornered her somewhere along the river, and, when she tried to ride off, he pulled her off her horse. She fought him, and I don't know if he raped her or not. She never said, figuring it wouldn't do no good to tell Red if he had.

"She rode in late that afternoon, bruised up some. Her shirt was torn. Later, when Max came in for supper, he had a lot of scratches on his face, so you can put two and two together. She told Red about fighting with Max, but, when he asked Max, he got a cock 'n' bull story about Kate falling off her horse and Max's face getting skinned up when he rode into the brush trying to roust out some steers that were hiding there. Red didn't believe Kate, which is the way I figured it would go. When she left on the stage the next morning to catch the train in Durango, she was crying and said she was never coming home. She did, of course, when she heard Red was dying, but I wish to hell she hadn't."

I sat there, listening, my hate for Max Landon becoming an acid in my belly, when the old man said: "He's coming, and he's riding in alone. You're gonna get your chance."

I got up, checked my gun, and eased it back into the holster, then pushed past Rogers who was still standing in the doorway. I had never in my life felt more like killing a man than I did at that moment.

# Chapter Nineteen

A man was coming in from the river. He was riding a big roan with the grace and ease of an experienced horseman. I walked toward the corral that held the horses, figuring that was where he'd stop. I didn't have any idea what Landon looked like, but I guess I expected to see a man with horns and a tail.

I didn't see that kind of man. I was standing about ten feet from the corral when he reined up and stepped down. He stood staring at me as if trying to determine whether I was an enemy or a friend, a medium-size man except that he was broader in the shoulders than most men, dark-haired with a brown mustache. I thought, in the first, quick glance that I had of him, that he was a very handsome man.

As prejudiced as I was, I had to admit there was only one feature that reminded me of the son-of-a-bitch that I knew he was. He had the coldest—no, iciest—eyes I had ever seen in any human being's face.

"You Max Landon?" I asked.

He nodded, those damned eyes probing me as if he still couldn't make up his mind just what kind of a huckleberry I was.

"You'll be interested to hear that Kate Muldoon is still alive," I said.

I figured he hadn't had time to hear what had happened to Jojo Birney. I thought that what I said would shake him up, but it didn't. He didn't bat an eye, but kept on staring at me as he said: "I'm glad to hear it."

"Jojo Birney's dead," I said. "I killed him when he was trying to murder Kate."

"That's good, too," he said, "though I don't know who this Birney *hombre* is you're talking about, or what he's got to do with me."

I had kept a tight rein on my temper up to that point, but I could feel it slipping. I said hotly: "You're a god-damned liar. You hired Birney to kill Kate. He lived long enough to tell me that."

My hunger to kill this man was almost uncontrollable, and I thought that what I said would make him go for his gun, but I couldn't see the slightest change in the expression in his eyes, and he made no motion for his gun. He had to be, I thought, the best poker player in the county.

"If somebody hired you to come here and kill me," he said in an even tone, "go ahead and get the job done, but I want you to know that, even though I don't like Kate very much, I don't dislike her enough to kill her."

I knew then I wasn't going to get a chance to kill him. He wasn't going to draw, and I couldn't kill a man, even Max Landon, who wouldn't defend himself. That was his protection, and he knew it. He was a good judge of men, and he was certain that, if I was a dry-gulcher, I'd have started shooting when he first stepped out of the saddle.

He turned to the corral gate to put his horse away. I started toward him, a thwarted rage boiling up in me that I could not control. I don't know what I intended to do, maybe beat hell out of him, but I didn't get the chance to do that. There was an instant when he moved in front of his horse to open the gate and was out of my sight. Now he wheeled to face me, his gun in his hand.

"I would not hesitate to shoot a man who wasn't drawing

on me," he said. "Now you best mount up and get to hell off my range."

"Your range!" I shouted at him, angrier than ever because he had drawn his gun without giving me a clue to his intentions, and I'd been caught flat-footed.

"My range," he said, nodding. "You seem to know what's going on. You didn't think the Diamond M was Kate's, did you?"

"She's Red Muldoon's daughter," I said hotly, knowing I'd better do what he said and ride out before he did shoot me. "She's his only kin."

"That's got nothing to do with it," he said. "The Diamond M is mine, and I aim to keep it."

"What I rode out here to tell you is that Judge Bailey will be reading the will tomorrow at three in his office. Kate will be there. The judge thought you should be there, too."

I did turn then and walked to my horse.

He said: "Hold on. I've got something to say to you."

I kept on walking, but I had trouble keeping from running. Suddenly I was scared. I guess that before this I had been carried away by my desire to kill Landon, and I wasn't really rational. I was now. Not that I was any less anxious to kill him, but I knew I wasn't going to get him to fight.

I had been foolish enough to think he had enough pride to be goaded into a fight, foolishness that could cost me my life. My only hope was that the cook was watching. I glanced toward the cook shack and saw Rogers standing in the doorway and guessed that was probably the reason that Landon hadn't shot me already.

I kept on walking. Before I reached my horse, he fired a shot, not at my back, but into the dirt beside me, the slug kicking up a small cloud of dust.

The echoes of that shot were still hammering at my ears

when he yelled: "Damn it, I said I had something to say."

I had played this as long as I could. It struck me as odd that I hadn't been scared when I had faced him and was trying to get him to fight, but I was scared now, so scared I had broken out in a cold sweat and I was trembling. I stopped and turned. I still could not see any change in his expression except that now his mouth held a hint of a smile.

He said: "I don't know what your game is or who the hell you are, but you'd better know that I worked my head off for Red Muldoon when he was alive. I have earned the Diamond M. Red wanted me to have it. He used to say I could run it the way he did and that was the only way to run an outfit like this. Kate don't know a damned thing about ranching. I have a right to this spread, and I aim to keep it. Now git."

I got. As I rode away, I felt a hot spot between my shoulder blades, then I glanced back at the cook shack and saw that Rogers was still standing there. I never thought I'd owe my life to a man who had simply stood watching me.

Landon wouldn't dare kill Rogers because he had no reason he could admit. If we had been alone, I'm sure he would have murdered me and hidden my body somewhere on the desert, and nobody except the coyotes that would probably have dug my body up would ever have known.

I didn't have anything to eat until I rode into Mrs. Horton's place late in the afternoon. I had barely cleared the mouth of the cañon and had come into sight from the front door when Kate ran out of the house toward me, her arms outstretched. I spurred my horse, reined up just before I reached her, and swung to the ground.

She fell into my arms, her arms around me, and began to cry. For a long time I stood motionless as we hugged each other, then Smith left the barn and strode toward me, a wide grin stretching his mouth farther than I had ever seen it stretched.

"Welcome back, son," Smith said, holding out his hand when he reached me.

I got my right arm free and gripped his hand. "I'm glad to be back," I said.

"Kate's been a mite worried," Smith said, "as any fool can see."

Kate had quit crying and tipped her head back. When I looked down at her, I saw the tears on her cheeks, and, if I had any doubts about her feelings for me, they were swept away.

The idea ran through my mind that it was lucky for her I felt the way I did, or she would have been deeply hurt. I was, I thought, her first and only love. I knew I had to give her more time, but her love was real, and I could afford to give her time.

She tried to say something, swallowed, and then blurted: "I wasn't just worried. I've been frantic."

"Go on into the house," Smith said. "I'll take care of your horse."

"I want to hear what happened," Kate said. "Did you see Judge Bailey?"

We walked into the house, holding hands. I said: "Yes. Everything's set. He'll read the will tomorrow at three in his office."

"Max?"

We walked into the house before I answered. The smell of frying steak came to me, and I didn't know if I could wait for supper or not. I was hungrier than I had realized. When Mrs. Horton heard us, she came out of the kitchen long enough to say: "We're glad you made it back alive and in one piece."

"So am I," I said.

"Kate was a mite fretful," Mrs. Horton said, and returned to the kitchen.

Kate released my hand and gripped my arm. "You don't want to tell me about Max, do you?"

The truth was, I didn't, or, rather, I didn't know how much to tell her. I didn't want to worry her. I simply needed a little time to think about what to say, so I put her off with: "I haven't had anything to eat since about dawn. Could you rustle me a cup of coffee?"

"Oh, I'm sorry." She ran into the kitchen and returned a moment later with a cup of black, steaming coffee. She said apologetically: "I didn't think about you being hungry. Aunt Becky will have supper on the table in a minute. Now tell me."

I sat down on the leather couch, and she dropped down beside me. She was fidgeting, and I knew she wasn't going to wait much longer, but I had to make a decision. I knew I wasn't going to tell her about killing the man in the hotel bar, or being locked up in Windy Holt's jail.

I sipped my coffee, then I said: "There isn't much to tell. I had a good visit with the judge. He was sure happy to hear you were alive and well. Naturally he was worried about the way you disappeared from your hotel room."

"He had a right to be," she said bitterly. "How did you like him?"

"I liked him fine," I said. "It's just that he's an old man, and he can't do much to enforce his decisions. He wants Landon in his office when he reads the will, so I rode out to the Diamond M and told him. I think he'll be there."

"What did you think of him?"

"He's smooth," I answered. "Smoother than I expected, and I guess that makes him all the more dangerous. He's going to give you trouble all the way."

"I know," she said.

Mrs. Horton appeared in the doorway saying that supper was ready, then looked around and asked: "Where's Smith? He knows enough to be here in time for a meal."

"Right here, ma'am," he said as he walked through the front door.

I ate enough for two men, and it wasn't until I sat back after two servings of rhubarb pie that I realized everybody had finished, and they were all watching me.

"I do like to see a man enjoy his food," Mrs. Horton said.

"Then I guess you enjoyed watching me eat," I said, and didn't apologize, thinking none was in order. "Now about tomorrow. We've got to be in Rolly by three o'clock. Judge Bailey will read the will. I don't know what will happen after that."

"I know Max Landon," Mrs. Horton said. "Your troubles will just be starting."

"That's the way I figured it," I said.

Kate stared at the table top. She said in a low tone: "I've thought about it ever since you left, Del. I don't want to lose the Diamond M, but I couldn't stand it if you were killed fighting Max for it."

"I aim to stay alive," I said. "Now I'm going to roll in."

Kate got up and came around the table and kissed me. Holding me in her arms, she said: "Thank you for what you've done for me. It's more than I can ever repay. I guess I keep saying that, but I just keep thinking it."

I looked down at her face, sad and worried and uncertain. Tomorrow, by this time, we would know how this was going to turn out, what our future was. Landon would not let it go if the will was in Kate's favor. Smith and I both might be dead. The Kid, too, if he turned up as he said he would. But I had no regrets. Something had happened to me during these few days I had been with Kate, something that was good and beautiful and would probably happen only once in a man's lifetime.

"Don't think about repaying me," I said. "I'd do this without pay."

I turned away quickly, giving Smith a tip of my head, and left the house. Smith recognized my signal and caught up with me before we reached the bunkhouse.

"I've got a hunch Kate don't know all that happened," he said.

"That's right. We're up against a stacked deck, John. At least as far as the county law is concerned. I don't know how many men Landon has on his payroll, or what they're like, but it's going to be long odds even with the Kid." I glanced at him as we went into the bunkhouse. "You want out?"

"Hell, no," he said, offhanded. "I don't have as much at stake as you do, but I signed on to see it through. Now tell me what happened, and don't make it sound easy."

I almost laughed when he said that. "Nothing easy about it," I said.

We sat down on our bunks, and I told him what had happened. When I finished, he said: "Since Landon's so hell-bent on hanging onto the spread regardless of Kate's rights, he won't want her showing up in the judge's office. How do you figure on getting her there alive?"

The possibility that Landon would ambush us on the road to Rolly hadn't really occurred to me before. I said: "I don't know. Got any ideas?"

"No, but I'll think on it." He paused, frowning thoughtfully. "Landon knows she's not in town now. He also knows where she is, or he wouldn't have sent Birney here to kill her. Now where does that leave us?"

162

"It leaves us getting shot out of our saddles on the road tomorrow," I said.

We went to bed, but I didn't sleep much. I don't think Smith did, either. When the triangle called us to breakfast, I didn't have any more idea about getting Kate into town alive than when we had gone to bed.

# Chapter Twenty

As I walked through the near pre-dawn darkness with Smith to the house, I said: "She's hitting that triangle a little earlier than usual."

He yawned and rubbed his eyes. "She sure as hell is. Wonder what's the matter with her that she couldn't sleep?"

"Dunno," I answered, "but I'll bet she's got some kind of a bee in her bonnet."

We went into the lamp-lit kitchen, washed, and sat down at the table as Kate came in. She said—"Good morning."—and we spoke to her. She looked tired. I didn't ask, but I had a hunch she hadn't slept very well, either.

Mrs. Horton brought a stack of flapjacks to the table, poured our coffee, and sat down. She looked at me belligerently as she said: "Before you cuss me for getting you up so early, I want to tell you why I done it. We should have figured on this last night, but I didn't think of it until I got to bed, and then I lay there turning and twisting something fierce. It hit me with a jolt that Max ain't gonna let Kate get to Rolly."

"John and I thought of that after we left last night," I said as I helped myself to the flapjacks, "but we couldn't figure out what to do about it. Chances are he'll set up an ambush between here and Rolly."

"But not on this end," she said. "I'm guessing he'll do it a few miles below Rolly. The cañon's narrow there, and he'd have a dozen places to hide and wait for you in the first five miles out of town."

I nodded, thinking she was probably right, and that Landon, careful man that he was, would pick a spot that held the least risk for his men. After three failures, he would send a crew to stop us and not depend on one man.

"You got an idea?" I asked.

She nodded. "It ain't a good one, but I know one thing for sure. You'll never in God's world go through the cañon and get Kate into town alive. Max will have his men hunkered down behind some rocks so you can't see 'em. When you get close enough, they'll just blow your heads off."

Kate put her coffee cup down and stared at Mrs. Horton. "Aunt Becky, are you saying we'd better not go?"

"No, you've got to go," Mrs. Horton said grimly, "but I am saying you'd better have a better notion than going up the main road along the river."

She was dragging this out, and I got a little testy. "Would you mind telling us what your idea is?"

"Don't get your feathers ruffled, young fellow," she snapped. "You ought to know by this time that I've got to do things my way and in my own time." She turned to Kate. "You remember the road to the Enterprise Mine?"

"Oh, sure," Kate said. "I've been up there several times with Daddy, but I was pretty young. He always had a small herd up there around the mine. It was pretty high, and the grass was always slow, so he was late getting the cattle up there. He'd make several trips during the summer to check on them, and he liked to take me along." She smiled a little bitterly, I thought. "That was when he still thought he could make a boy out of me."

"It's a rough climb to where the mine is," Mrs. Horton said. "You've got to go up almost to timberline, but, once you get there, you can swing left to the North Star Mine. It's purty easy riding the rest of the way into Rolly. The road drops almost straight down to town." She looked at me triumphantly. "What do you think of it?"

"It'll work if Kate knows the way," I said. "Landon won't be looking for us to come that way."

Mrs. Horton nodded. "Not likely he will. Now eat up and get moving. It'll take you a lot longer than if you stay on the road."

"I've only been to the North Star once, but I remember the road," Kate said. "It sure is steep once you start down from the mine. Daddy said he always wondered how they got their machinery and timber up that grade."

"All right, then," Mrs. Horton said. "The main trouble is it ain't much of a road to the Enterprise. You'll have to look for it, because they've done some grading where it leaves the main road. Now saddle up."

Within a matter of minutes we were in the narrow cañon that led to the river. When we reached it, we turned upstream. I rode about fifty yards in front of Kate, thinking we might not have guessed right about where Landon would set his trap. The man was unpredictable. That was one thing we could count on.

By riding ahead I expected to draw the first fire, if we did run into his ambush, and that might give Kate and Smith a chance to ride back down the cañon, or at least find shelter. Not that either would do much good because Landon would go after them. With me out of the picture, and with the odds four or five to one, Smith wouldn't have much chance of getting Kate back to Mrs. Horton's place.

The sun was barely high enough to throw its morning light into the bottom of the cañon when Kate called: "I think you passed it, Del."

I had been getting worried because I knew we were not more than six or seven miles from Rolly, and the cañon was beginning to narrow, so we were in the area where Landon was likely to have stationed his men. I turned back, carefully watching the east side of the road for a break that might indicate where the old mine road had turned up the mountain.

I couldn't find any trace of the break I was looking for, but, when I reached Kate, she pointed to a steep-walled cañon farther up the slope. "I'm sure the road to the mine is in that cañon, but it's like Aunt Becky said. They've done some grading along here, and they've cut away the dirt where the old mine road led off of this one."

"There's nothing along here that looks like a road," I said, not sure that she was right.

"I said it had been changed," she said, "but I'm sure that's where the road is. It hasn't been used for fifteen years or more, so it's probably just a trail by now." She pointed across the river to an outcropping of rock on the other side. "The reason I'm sure this is the place is that Daddy always called that formation over yonder the Old Man. He had more imagination than I did. I never could see an old man in that rock."

"The underbrush grows up in fifteen years," Smith said, "and, since they've done so much scraping along here, they've wiped out where the mine road came out. Kate's probably right."

I couldn't argue any more. We had to get into that side cañon to find out, so I nodded and spurred my horse up the next bank. It was steep. The ground was soft and gave under my horse's hoofs, but he snorted, muscles straining, and within a few minutes we reached a gentler slope. I pulled up and waited for the others. Smith followed me, then Kate, and, when they were beside me, I said: "I hope we don't hit anything steeper than that."

"We won't," Kate said, and pointed into the aspen grove ahead of us. "You can see wheel ruts if you look close."

It struck me she was using her imagination, but I rode on up the mountain and presently came into a clearing where I could plainly see the ruts. A few minutes later we were in the narrow cañon we had seen from the road, and here the ruts were even deeper.

The climb was easier from this point. We had to stop often to blow the horses, and, when we came out of the cañon, we were close to timberline. There was no timber here except for a scattering of small, wind-bent trees, but the grass was good, and I saw why Red Muldoon had brought cattle here for the summer months. I was surprised that there weren't any here now.

The buildings of the Enterprise Mine were directly ahead of us. They showed years of neglect: broken windows, doors sagging, rusting machinery, roofs caved in from weight of winter snows, all darkened by sun and wind to a dingy gray. I always had a strange feeling when I was around old mines, as if they were graveyards of men's dreams. The dreams about the Enterprise must have been big, I thought, judging from the amount of machinery scattered around and the size and variety of buildings.

When we pulled up and looked around, Kate read my mind, I guess, because she said: "Daddy told me, when we were here one time, that the owners spent more than a million dollars developing the mine. He didn't know how much silver was found, but the company went broke and a lot of Eastern investors lost everything. He'd heard some sad stories of widows and old people who got taken in and lost their life savings."

"An old story," I said.

"Greed," Smith said.

Kate looked at him thoughtfully. "I don't agree with that, John. Is it greed for a person to want an easier life? Those people thought they'd get it from the earnings on their investment."

He shrugged. "Call it gullibility. Nobody who has a brain in his head would invest in a mine unless he could afford to lose his investment."

"That's a logical thing for you to say," Kate snapped with more feeling than usual, "but, if you have lived in poverty and see a way to get out of that kind of life, I say it's a dream."

"If anybody spends his money on a dream, I still say he's gullible," Smith said.

"John Smith, you are an exasperating man," Kate said angrily. "Didn't you ever invest in a dream?"

He was silent for a moment as he stared at the jagged, snow-covered peaks to the west, his face very grave. Finally he said: "Yes, Kate, I invested in a dream. Not money. Just my life, and I can tell you I was gullible."

The argument was getting out of hand, I thought. Besides, the sun had gone under a cloud, and a cold wind suddenly raced across the mountain tops and drove its icy knife into us. It was no place to sit and talk.

"We'd better ride," I said, and headed north.

We made better time after leaving the Enterprise. There never had been a road across here, but we took Mrs. Horton's words and followed a direct course to the north, at times weaving around rock outcroppings or dropping into shallow ravines and climbing out again.

Once we were forced around a rock pillar to the edge of a sharp slope that broke off to the west and formed what was close to a sheer cliff. I wasn't sure this was the best way to go, but we would have had to go out of our way to swing

169

back and would have lost time. Besides, we found ourselves on a ledge that would have made it difficult to turn. We took a chance, and in a few more minutes the ledge widened, and I was able to swing right and, after a short, steep climb, reach a gentle slope that enabled us again to ride directly north.

Kate was right behind me, but I was surprised to look back and see that Smith had stopped on the narrow ledge and was staring into the cañon below him. I had not wanted to stop there, partly because I was worried about the ledge petering out, but mostly because I never felt comfortable standing at the edge of nothing and looking down into it. I thought I had seen some rugged country in Montana, but the Colorado Rockies made it look like a series of hills.

"What's the matter with John?" I asked Kate. "That's no place to stop to view the scenery."

"What *is* the matter with him, Del?" Kate responded. "I never heard him talk like that before, about being gullible and investing his life and all that."

"You don't really know John," I said. "He holds a lot of things inside and doesn't talk about them. He killed a man once, and he's been on the run ever since."

"Oh," she said. "I didn't know."

I let it go at that, thinking that Smith would tell the whole story if and when he wanted to. He joined us a moment later, a sour expression on his face.

"You should have had a good look into the cañon," he said. "We were right over the narrowest part of it. I could see the road, and the river looked like a silver ribbon."

"I didn't figure there was anything down there I wanted," I said.

"You're right about that," he said. "You don't want what's down there. Looked like about six men, all hunkered down behind some rocks right at the foot of the cliff below us. I couldn't see for sure how many men there were, but I did count six horses."

"Well, I'm not surprised," I said, mentally thanking Mrs. Horton. "Landon is going to be disappointed."

We rode on, reaching the North Star Mine within the hour. No rusting machinery here, no broken windows, no sagging doors. Everything looked as if the mine had been closed yesterday. Smoke rose from the chimney of one of the shacks, and I guessed the owners kept a watchman up here, probably planning to open the mine as soon as the company raised more capital. I thought about what Smith had said regarding gullibility, and told myself that hope is slow to die where gold or silver is concerned.

The door on the shack with the smoke banged open and a man stepped out, carrying a rifle on the ready. For one scared moment I thought of going for my gun, thinking that Landon had stationed a man up here to watch for us, but he made no hostile motion, just stood watching us as we rode by.

The road to Rolly was plain, looking as if it had been used recently. We started downslope, and soon found ourselves looking down on Rolly; the buildings reminded me of a toy village I'd had as a child. Another hour put us in town.

# Chapter Twenty-One

We entered Main Street at its upper end and turned south on it, my gaze sweeping the street. No one was in sight. I had never seen much activity on Rolly's Main Street, but today it was more deserted than usual, with only one horse, a big roan, tied in front of the stable. A couple of dogs dozed in the afternoon sun, and several chickens scratched in the street in front of the livery stable, but, aside from that, a man would think Rolly was a ghost town.

I had a hunch something was wrong. It was too quiet here, the quiet of death. I kept studying the street as we rode, wondering if Landon had set up a trap for us here in town, but I didn't consider that likely. Too many people would see it, and that wasn't good business for even a man like Landon. There was a point beyond which he could not go no matter how thoroughly he had cowed the people.

Men could be hidden on the roofs and I wouldn't see them, but we had to get rid of our horses and eat dinner in time to reach Judge Bailey's office by three. That, I thought, might be a little tricky, having to cross Main Street.

I glanced at Smith, and he gave me a bare half-inch nod, understanding the risk we were taking. Fortunately, the livery stable was at the upper end of the block. We swung close to the boardwalk on the eastern side of the street and turned through the archway of the stable as soon as we reached it.

I dismounted and gave Kate a hand. The stableman came out of the rear of the building, then stood staring at

Kate as if he could not believe what he saw.

"What's the matter with you, Andy?" Kate asked. "I'm not a ghost, if that's what you're thinking."

He swallowed, glanced at me, then Smith, and finally brought his gaze back to Kate. He said: "I just didn't expect to see you. That's all."

"You'd better explain that," I said.

He took the reins of Kate's horse and started to lead him into a stall, but, when I took a step toward him, he stopped. "Well, damn it, I don't know what's going on. All I know is that we've had men shot to death and that ain't happened in Rolly since the boom days. Another thing. The talk is that Max Landon is gonna clean your plow for you if and when you show up in town. Maybe it's just talk. I didn't hear Max say it, and his boys didn't leave their horses here when they got to town."

"Then that's why folks are staying in," I said.

He nodded. "The town's buzzing with all kinds of gossip. I don't know that Landon said anything, but then he ain't much for talking."

"Any of his men in town?" I asked.

"All of 'em rode in early this morning, then rode out again." He swallowed, then blurted: "One of 'em is still here. That's his roan you seen in the street. Name's Hawk Sloan." He swallowed again, then said as if he knew he shouldn't be saying it: "Kate, I've knowed you clean back to when your ma was alive. I sure want you to get what's yours, but Max, he ain't one to overlook it if a man don't take his side."

"I know, Andy," Kate said. "Don't do anything that will make him mad at you."

"One thing," Andy glanced at me, then at my gun, and finally brought his eyes back to my face. "This Sloan. They say he's a gunfighter. I hope you can take him."

He led Kate's horse along the runway and into a stall.

I said: "Let's go put the feedbag on. We won't have time to get dinner if we don't get to it."

We walked out of the stable, glancing up and down the street as we moved through the archway, then up at the roofs on the opposite side of the street. I wondered why we did. Half a dozen men could be hunkered down behind the false fronts ready to fill us full of lead any time we were in the street, and we wouldn't see them.

"You know this Hawk Sloan?" I asked Kate.

She shook her head. "He's a new man. It's my guess all of them are." She gripped my arm. "Del, I'm ready to let this go."

"We've gone this far," I said. "We're not backing out now. It's more than you getting your spread. At least it is for me. Besides, if we left, Landon would have you followed. He can't stop until you're dead."

Smith nodded. "That's right. Besides, I never like to leave a job half done."

We turned off the street into the hotel lobby. We had almost reached the door of the dining room when I heard a whoop and turned to see the Kid run out of the bar and head for us. He pumped my hand and then Smith's as if he hadn't seen us for a year. He said: "By God, I thought it was time you was getting here. I've been hearing some funny talk since I rode into town." He looked at Kate and got red in the face. He took his hat off and kind of bowed in her direction as if not knowing how he should act. "Excuse me for cussin', ma'am. I didn't aim to do it in front of you."

She laughed and, putting her hands up to his head, drew it down and kissed him on the cheek. "It's all right. I've heard a little cussing in my life. Daddy was known for his cussing."

"Aw, you're joshing now," the Kid said.

"Let's eat," I broke in impatiently. "My tapeworm's been hollering for the last hour."

We went into the dining room and gave our order. The Kid had already eaten, so he was satisfied with a cup of coffee. As soon as the waitress left, Smith asked: "Where have you been, Kid? Robbing a bank?"

"Hell, no," the Kid said as if Smith had made a reasonable statement. "Bank robbing is a two-man job. I been in Ophir. I was heading for Telluride, but I got into an all-night poker game before I got there. I done purty good, too." He dug a handful of gold coins out of his pocket and showed them to us. "It's the most *dinero* I've had since . . ."—he was about to say, I thought, since he and Smith had robbed a bank, but caught himself in time and finished with—"since I had that big hand in Baggs."

"Now about that talk you've been hearing?" I asked.

Our oyster soup came, and I dropped a handful of crackers into it and stirred. The Kid was uneasy about something. He sipped his coffee and set the cup back in its saucer. His gaze moved to Kate, to his cup, then to Kate again.

"It's all right," I said. "Kate's got a right to know what's going on."

"Well, like I said," the Kid muttered, looking down at his cup, "the talk was by some town men in the hotel bar. They'd been drinking, and they was scared. One of 'em . . . and I don't know what business he was in . . . kept saying Max Landon could keep this county going just like Red Muldoon used to do. On the other hand, if Muldoon's girl got the Diamond M, business would be worse than it is now."

"That's a terrible thing to say," Kate cried indignantly.

"What's owning the Diamond M got to do with the county's business?"

Before the Kid could answer, I saw a man get up from a table near the window and walk to the desk in the lobby. He was a tall, narrow-hipped man with a long nose that had enough hump in it to make him look a little like a hawk. He wore one gun on his left side, butt forward, the holster thonged down the way gunfighters do. There was no mistaking a man like that.

There was, I thought, enough lawlessness in the West for a man like this to prosper, particularly in any area that was torn between two warring factions such as cattlemen and sheepmen. His presence in Rolly was proof of what Max Landon expected or, at least, thought might happen here.

I don't know why he expected one small young woman to give him that kind of trouble. He had no way of knowing she would hire a crew of bodyguards. Maybe he was afraid his high-handed methods would turn the community against him, and he wanted to keep them terrified enough to stop any resistance before it got organized.

I nodded to the man who had stopped at the desk and was talking to the clerk. I said: "That's our Hawk Sloan your friend Andy was talking about or I miss my guess."

"That's who he is, all right," the Kid said. "He was in the bar last night, and I heard him called that. You know him?"

I shook my head. "No, but we heard in the livery stable that he was Landon's insurance. He talk any in the bar?"

"No. Just sat at a table drinking." The Kid leaned back in his chair, a half smile touching the corners of his mouth. "You know, Del, I figure I can take him."

"You may get a chance," I said.

The Kid sat facing a window. Now he straightened up,

surprised at something he saw in the street. "What do you know about that," he said. "He's leaving town."

"Going which way?"

"South."

"Now that's downright interesting," Smith said softly. "We'll be seeing Landon and his crew before long."

Kate had been looking at the Kid so intently I wondered if she was aware of what she was doing. Now she said: "In all that talk you heard in the bar, did anybody say I had a right to my daddy's ranch?"

"Yeah, one man did," the Kid answered. "A fat old jasper. Had a white beard."

I nodded at Kate. "The banker."

"Adam Jessup," she agreed. "Well, I'm glad I have one friend in town who would stick up for me."

"You've got more than that," I told her. "It's just that they're afraid to say anything that might get them in trouble with Landon. Once we take care of him, you'll see."

Our order had come, and she sat looking at her plate. Finally she said in an unhappy tone: "What kind of friends are they who won't defend you?"

"Not the best," I agreed, "but they're afraid, and, when a man's afraid, he's not his usual self. On the other hand, Judge Bailey and Jessup have openly sided you."

"I'm thankful for them," she said.

I glanced at the big clock on the wall near the lobby door. It said twenty minutes till three. I said: "We'd better get a move on. I don't want to get caught on this side of the street when Landon and his crew ride into town."

We hastily finished eating and left the dining room. Kate asked: "Will you pay for our meals, Del? I'll see you get your money back." She was barely able to smile as she added: "It'll be the day I get my inheritance."

"You'll get it someday whether we do the job or not," I said. "The will has to favor you. Your daddy couldn't have made it any other way, and a man like Landon can't go on defying the law forever."

"Someday," she said bitterly. "It never should come down to that."

I nodded, understanding how she felt, and paid the hotel clerk. I leaned across the desk and asked in a low tone: "That was Hawk Sloan you were talking to, wasn't it?" He nodded, eyeing me warily, and when I asked—"What were you talking about?"—he backed away from his desk and started edging along the wall so he was close to a hall and could make a run for it.

I drew my gun and eared back the hammer. As I lined it on his chest, I said: "I don't usually shoot unarmed men, but, then, I'm not sure you are a man. A weasel, maybe, and it's always open season on weasels."

He was a small man with a nervous tic in the left side of his mouth. Now the muscle began jerking violently, his furtive manner reminding me more of a weasel than ever. I heard the Kid snicker behind me. He said: "You're right, Del. He does look like a weasel for a fact. Ain't that gonna be the fifth notch on your gun?"

"No, the sixth," Smith corrected. "Remember that big *hombre* in Baggs that Del knocked over? He had five bullet holes in him before he hit the floor as I remember it."

"Oh, yeah," the Kid said. "I clean forgot about him."

I thought the clerk was going to fall right through the wall. He looked past me at Kate. "You wouldn't let him kill, me, would you, Miss Muldoon?"

"I can't always handle him, Weasel," Kate said. "When he gets like this, nobody can."

The clerk swallowed, his Adam's apple bobbing up and

down in his neck. "Sloan just asked me if you was Kate Muldoon?"

"What'd you tell him?" I demanded.

"I told him she was," the clerk said. "She is, too. I'd know her anywhere, even if she has been gone for a year. Besides, she registered here one night, and then she disappeared."

"What happened to her?"

"Dunno. Come morning, she wasn't in her room. Just went off and left her suitcase. I told the sheriff about it."

I turned away, disgusted. As we crossed the street, I said: "I'm a tougher man than I realized."

The Kid guffawed. "You ain't doing bad."

"You called him Weasel," I said to Kate. "You just say that because of what I said?"

"Of course not," she said. "He's been called that as long as I can remember."

# Chapter Twenty-Two

When we reached the bank, I said: "Let's go in. John, I want you and the Kid to watch the street. Kate and I are going to Judge Bailey's office."

"What do you want us to do?" the Kid asked eagerly, too eagerly, I thought.

"Just watch," I said. "We're not going to jump the gun. Maybe we won't have to."

"The hell we won't," the Kid said. "We're going to have some fun out of this."

"Landon will come up to Bailey's office, and I can handle him," I said, ignoring the Kid. "If he brings any of his men with him, you'd better come on up, but I don't think he will."

Adam Jessup rose from where he had been sitting at his desk and came to us in long strides. He said, as he extended his hand to Kate: "You sure are a sight for sore eyes, girl. We were all worried about you when you disappeared from your hotel room."

"I'm glad to be alive," Kate said as she shook hands. "You've met Mister Delaney, I believe."

"Yes, I have," Jessup said.

"I want you to meet his friends who are also working for me. Mister Smith and the Kid."

He shook hands with both, saying: "If you're on Kate's side, I'm glad you're here. I don't know what to expect from Landon this afternoon, but I did hear some ominous rumors last night."

"He didn't expect us to get here," Kate said, "and I'll have to admit I wasn't sure we would."

Jessup nodded. "Max is never one to take chances. Mister Delaney told me he had sent men to kill you. I know he wants the Diamond M so bad that he's a little crazy, but I never dreamed he was that crazy."

I didn't sense the fear in Jessup that I had the other time I had talked to him, and I was surprised he had spoken up for Kate in the hotel bar the night before. Somewhere he had found courage, maybe from Judge Bailey, or maybe just from the fact that somebody else was willing to fight for Kate.

I glanced up at the clock on the wall. It was five minutes before three. I said to Kate: "We'd better get upstairs."

She nodded, and turned toward the door.

I hesitated, looking at the Kid. He still had that look in his eyes, almost a crazy expression, reminding me of a feisty dog that was ready to take on another dog and was eager for the fight. I opened my mouth to tell him to take it easy, but I turned away without saying a word. I'd been with the Kid long enough to know that he obeyed no voice but his own. That, I thought, was the reason he was riding the Outlaw Trail and that he'd keep on riding it to the end.

I followed Kate up the stairs, unable to throw off an uneasy feeling about the Kid. His wild eagerness might get us into more trouble than we could handle, enough to spoil everything we'd planned, but I didn't say it to the Kid. There just wasn't a damned thing I could do about it.

I went into Judge Bailey's office behind Kate. He was standing by the window looking down into Main Street. He turned when he heard the door open and welcomed Kate with open arms. She hugged him and cried a little, and the judge dabbed at his eyes with a white handkerchief. There was, I thought, a deep bond of affection between them.

"I'm so glad to see you, Kate," the judge said. "More than I can say. After what Delaney told me about the attempts on your life, I was afraid you'd never get here."

"We almost didn't," Kate said.

"What happened?"

"We guessed Max would stop us somewhere on the road between here and Aunt Becky's place," Kate answered, "so we went up the mountain to the Enterprise and across the North Star, then came into town at the upper end of Main Street."

The judge shook his head, swearing softly. "I figured he'd do something to stop you. I saw Hawk Sloan leave town a while ago in a hell of a hurry. He'll be fetching Max and the boys back." Suddenly he seemed to be aware of my presence and nodded at me. "Glad to see you, too, Delaney. You won't be surprised to hear that Windy Holt has gone fishing."

"No," I said, "it's what I expected."

Kate came to me and put an arm around me. "I don't know what controls our destiny, Judge, but I believe it had to be my guardian angel that sent Del along the hall just in time to hear me scream. It was timed almost to the second. I got out one good yell just before he pressed the pillow over my face. After that, I couldn't even breathe."

"These things happen," the judge agreed. "Call it luck or a guardian angel. Either way, we have to admit that there is a law beyond our conscious minds that dictates the events of our lives."

He turned back toward the window and walked to it. Kate looked at me and smiled, and I felt a wave of love for her that was different from anything I had ever experienced in my life.

"Kate," I said in a low tone, "do you know me well enough to put up with me the rest of my life?"

"Of course, I do," she said. "Sometimes months pass and nothing happens, but there are other times when a year of experience is packed into a few days. That's what's happened to us. If you feel the way I do, I'm glad it happened."

"Oh, I'm glad," I said. "Sometimes I wonder if it . . . ?"

"They're here," the judge interrupted.

We walked to where the judge stood and looked over his shoulder. Six men had ridden into town from the south, Max Landon in the lead. They reined up in front of the hotel, dismounted, and tied, then went in without as much as a glance along the street.

"That one right behind Max is Hawk Sloan," the judge said. "He's the one to watch. He's only been working for Max a few weeks. Nobody knows where he came from, but he's got the marks of a gunfighter all over him."

"Then Landon was looking for trouble," I said.

"It's about the only conclusion you can draw," Bailey agreed. "He knew Kate had more right to the Diamond M than he did, so he must have figured that he needed someone who could defy the law, such as it is around here, and make it stick."

"I thought Landon had the county buffaloed a long time ago," I said.

A small smile touched the corners of the judge's mouth. "He did, but there was one difference. I never took Max for a very brave man, so he needed someone who was willing to die. I've seen men like Sloan, willing to gamble their lives for pay. Max had to consider the possibility that somebody would fight for Kate."

I thought about it as we stood there. I'd had that feeling about Landon from the time I'd braced him in front of the

Diamond M corral. Since he hadn't fought then, as most men would have done, he wasn't likely to fight now, so he'd be counting on Sloan.

Apparently the judge was thinking along the same line when he asked: "What are your plans, Delaney?"

"I don't know," I said. "I know what I want to do, but killing Sloan won't do the job."

"No, and, anyhow, I'd hate to see you tackle him," the judge said. "I don't take you for a gunfighter. Sloan is."

I nodded. "He'd kill me. Anyhow, Landon is the man I want. It doesn't do any good to cut off a branch when you've got to take a tree out by the roots."

Kate gripped my arm. "But how are you going to get at Max as long as he hides behind Sloan?"

"I haven't figured that out," I said.

"Here he comes," the judge said, and glanced at his watch. "Just ten minutes late."

We watched Landon cross the street to the bank, walking in long strides, shoulders back, Stetson cocked at a jaunty angle, and rounding the corner of the bank at the foot of the stairs. The judge walked to his desk and stood back of his chair. Kate and I remained by the window facing the door, my right hand close to the butt of my gun, Kate still gripping my arm.

I didn't think Landon would draw on me here, but I couldn't risk being caught off guard. I was confident of one thing: if Landon had an advantage of any kind, he'd use it.

We heard him open the door at the head of the stairs, come on along the hall to Bailey's office, then saw him stop in the doorway, staring at me. He just stood there motionless for quite a while. I saw a series of emotions cross his face, first astonishment, then questioning, and finally rage that turned his face a sort of brick red.

"Come in and have a chair, Max," the judge said.

He still didn't move as his gaze turned to Bailey. He asked in a rough tone: "What kind of a god-damned joke are you playing on me? I want this huckleberry out of here. He don't belong in this room when the will is being read, so get him out."

"He has every right to be here," Kate said, a steely quality in her voice I had not heard before. "He and I will be married soon. He's staying."

"You turned me down to marry a saddle bum who probably has the law on his tail?" Landon asked as if he couldn't believe it.

"He's not a saddle bum," Kate cried indignantly. "If there ever was a saddle bum, you were him when you rode into the Diamond M that time, and Daddy took you in. Now you repay him by trying to murder me."

"I don't know what you're talking about," Landon shouted as if angered by the accusation.

"Come in and shut the door," Bailey said testily, "and sit down. Delaney here represents Kate, and, if she wants him to stay, he can. Now you either keep a civil tongue in your head or leave, and Kate can listen to the will by herself."

Landon hesitated, his eyes filled with murderous hatred as he stared at me, then he slowly shut the door and moved toward Bailey's desk. As he dropped into a chair across from Bailey, the judge motioned for Kate to take the second chair beside Landon's. I remained by the window.

The judge opened a drawer, took out a long envelope, and shut the drawer. He opened the envelope and drew out a single sheet of paper. He unfolded it, ran a hand over to smooth it, and cleared his throat as he picked up a pair of gold-rimmed spectacles and put them on.

"Red left a very simple will, and there can be no doubt of his intentions," Bailey said. "Aside from his personal possessions, he had only two assets, the ranch and his savings accounts plus some money in a checking account to handle the operating expenses of the Diamond M." He nodded at Kate. "Of course, Max has had access to the checking account, so he knows exactly what there is in it. At the moment I don't know."

He lifted the sheet of paper and started to read. "I, Patrick Muldoon, commonly known as Red Muldoon, being of a sound mind, do hereby leave my property, land, stock, and cash to my beloved daughter, Katharine Ann Muldoon. It is my wish that Max Landon who has been a son to me will continue to be employed by Katharine as foreman of the Diamond M and, in time, will become a full partner. In the event of Katharine's death, the entire estate will go to Max Landon. Signed, Patrick Muldoon."

Bailey folded the will and slipped it back into its envelope. He removed his glasses and leaned back, his gaze on Landon. "If Kate does not want to employ you, and I understand she does not, you will be required to vacate the premises within twenty-four hours. I might add that, in view of your recent attempts to murder Kate, she is legally and morally justified in not keeping you on as foreman."

Landon sat as if frozen, staring at Bailey. "You never have liked me, you old son-of-a-bitch. You wrote that will, and he signed it. Red never would have made a will like that if he had been of a sound mind."

"On the contrary, Max," Bailey said, apparently unruffled, "I would have written a very different will and in different terminology, but you know as well as I do that Red was a very strong-minded man. He came in here almost a year ago and told me exactly what he wanted and how he

186

wanted it said, so that is the way I wrote it, had it witnessed, and filed it."

Landon rose slowly, so furious he was trembling. "I don't believe it. As for me vacating the premises, you try to make me do it." He turned his head to glare at me. "I'll promise you one thing, drifter. You'll never leave town alive."

He wheeled and stomped out of the office, slamming the door behind him. For a moment none of us spoke, or even breathed, I think, then I walked to the desk and said: "Judge, that is the damnedest will I ever heard. It's an invitation to murder."

Bailey nodded. "I know. I even told Red that, and he got sore at me for hinting that Max would ever injure Kate."

I looked at her and saw that her head was bowed and that she was silently crying.

# Chapter Twenty-Three

I stood at the window, looking down into the street. I just couldn't get over thinking about a man who was supposed to be smart writing a will that would put his daughter in danger. Granted, he was blind to Landon's faults, but still any man in his right mind would have to consider the possibility such a will might turn his foreman's mind toward murder.

In his right mind! That had to be the explanation. Red Muldoon had become senile. Kate had dropped hints that her father had changed. He must have been close to being senile when Landon had attacked Kate, perhaps raped her, and he had refused to believe what she had said.

I watched Landon as he came into sight below me and crossed to the hotel. He walked in long, angry strides, stirring the dust each time he slammed his boot soles into the street. He disappeared into the hotel lobby, and I thought about his threat that I would never leave town alive. I wondered what his next move would be.

"Delaney!" the judge called.

I turned. Kate had stopped crying and was dabbing at her eyes with a handkerchief. She looked up at me and smiled. Not much of a smile, not the warm, loving smile I had seen so many times, but I knew she meant it for that kind of a smile.

"I'm sorry to be such a baby, Del," she said, "but I just couldn't help it. I'm glad Daddy was himself enough to leave the estate to me, but he wasn't himself enough to figure out that his will was exactly what you said it was. An invitation to murder."

"He must have been senile," I said.

"No, not senile in the medical sense," the judge said defensively, guessing, I thought, that I was going to cuss him out for writing the will, "but he wasn't right in the head, either. He was obsessed by his fear that the Diamond M would cease to be a visible ranch. By visible, I mean a ranch that turned a profit and also gave the owner power and prestige. In a small, poor county like this, it all goes together if the owner is ambitious and aggressive enough to seek that power. Red was, and he knew Max would be."

"And a daughter wouldn't be," Kate said bitterly.

"You're a woman," Bailey said, "and Red was not a man to see women as being aggressive."

"Or ambitious," Kate added.

Bailey shrugged. "I think that explains why Red, old and sick and knowing he would die soon, hoped that you would keep Max on as foreman or in time marry him. Of course, if you did die, he wanted Max to have the ranch." He turned his gaze to me. "Delaney, I know Max pretty well. He becomes a madman when he's furious, and I never saw him more furious than he was just now. It's my guess that the second you go down the stairs into the street, they'll start shooting. Of course, they'll claim they had no intention of killing Kate, that she just happened to become a victim of the fighting that they started to keep the peace in the community. Since Holt isn't around, Max would claim he felt it was up to him."

"I can't stay here," I said.

"No," Bailey agreed, "but what are you going to do?"

"My two friends are in the bank," I said. "I want to reach

them before we get into a fight. There is a back door to the bank, isn't there?"

Bailey nodded. "It's usually unlocked, but how are you going to get to the back door without being seen?"

"The foot of the stairs is not right at the corner of the building," I said. "If I turn toward the stairs the instant I hit the ground, I don't think they'll spot me."

"And after that?" Bailey asked.

"I don't know," I admitted. "We've got to figure out some way to root Landon out of the hotel."

Kate rose. "I'm going with you."

When I looked at her and saw the determined set of her jaw, I knew there was no use to argue with her. She could, on occasion, be a very stubborn and independent woman, so I nodded, and we left the judge's office.

We walked along the hall to the door at the head of the stairs. We hesitated, looking at each other, Kate gripping my arm. It struck me that this was the day we had been waiting for, actually the moment, and still I did not have a clear notion what I would do.

"I love you," I said.

She drew her hand away from my arm and lifted both hands to the back of my head and drew it down to kiss me, then she said: "I love you, too. You get angry when I say I belong to you, but I do, and I have from the first moment you saved my life. I can't lose you now."

I held her close for a moment, then said—"You won't lose me."—and I wished to hell I felt as confident as my words sounded. "You go ahead and turn to the rear without showing yourself if you can. If they are watching and catch a glimpse of you, you'll be out of their sight before they can have time to shoot."

I opened the door, and we went down the stairs, Kate

turning quickly when she reached the ground just as I told her to. I didn't go clear to the bottom, but vaulted the railing from the third step above the ground. I wasn't sure how much they could see from the lobby of the hotel, but I knew that, if they had caught a glimpse of Kate, they'd be ready for me, and I didn't want to take that chance.

When we reached the back corner of the bank building, I peered cautiously around it. I had no idea whether Landon had thought of us going around this way or not, but I realized he might have stationed some of his men back here in the alley to cut us down.

I saw no one. Nothing moved except a black cat that was walking slowly toward us. There was the usual clutter of chunks of wood and tin cans and weeds, all typical of an alley in a small town, but no sign of human life. I wanted two or three minutes to be sure, probing as well as I could any possible hiding place a man might find, but there simply was no such place along this alley unless he was in one of the houses that butted against the alley, and that seemed unlikely.

"All right," I said, "let's move."

We rounded the corner of the building and ran to the back door. I put a hand on the knob to open the door, then I froze, suddenly remembering the feisty, excited look in the Kid's eyes. He was primed for trouble, trigger-happy, and I thought the sound of the opening of the door would probably bring a slug from his gun before he saw who had come in.

I knocked, then stood to one side as I opened the door, calling: "It's us!"

"Come in," Smith called back, "and join the tea party!"

The moment we stepped into the bank, I knew my fears had been justified. The Kid stood with his back to one of the street windows, his cocked gun in his hand. He grinned sheepishly as he eased the hammer down and slid his Colt into leather.

"Good thing you knocked," the Kid said. "I'm a little jumpy, I guess, but I thought that bunch of hardcases might be trying to run a sandy on us."

"Landon doesn't know you're here or even who you are," I said as I walked toward the front of the bank. "He does know that Kate and I were upstairs in the judge's office, but I don't think they saw us come down the stairs. The judge figured Landon would mow us down the minute we showed ourselves in the street."

"He wouldn't gun a woman down in the plain view of the whole town," Smith objected.

"He would," Jessup said, "figuring he could claim it was an accident."

"That's about what the judge said," I told the banker, surprised that the two men would come so near saying the same thing about Landon.

"We know Max," Jessup said. "The one thing you don't understand and probably can't is the insane desire Max has to own the Diamond M. He's been in here a couple of times asking for a loan to buy new stock to upgrade the Diamond M herd, as if the outfit already belonged to him. I told him he'd have to deal through Kate, and he brushed me off as if Kate had nothing to do with it." Jessup stroked his beard thoughtfully, looking at Kate. He went on: "It is extraordinary, because I had always thought Max was a fairly rational man." He hesitated, then asked: "What did the will say?"

"I get everything," Kate said, "but, in the event of my death, it all goes to Max."

"The hell," Smith said as if he couldn't believe it. "No wonder Landon has been so anxious to kill you."

"I knew Daddy had gone downhill lately," Kate said. "Some of his last letters were not very coherent, but I didn't think he'd leave the kind of will that he did. I've been wondering if Max knew all the time what was in the will."

"He sure seemed to think he was going to get the estate," Jessup said. "Well, this is the showdown. It's more than just you, or Delaney. All of us in the county will be affected, all but Windy Holt."

"Whatever happens, you stay out of it," Kate said.

I noticed that Jessup had leaned a shotgun against the wall by the door. I asked, nodding at it: "What are you going to do with your Greener?"

"I'm an old man," Jessup said, "and I don't see very well at a distance, but, if I'm needed, I'll do what I can. You may get more help than you expected, Delaney. And don't tell me what to do, Kate."

"I just don't want you to get hurt," Kate said, and then sighed. "All right, Adam. I guess you've got along all right without my advice."

I knew she was pleased. So was I. I had the idea that the whole town had been so buffaloed by Landon that no one would raise a hand for Kate, but I'd been wrong. I suspected that the judge might have a Winchester on the ready upstairs beside a window. Perhaps there were others, but it still came down to me and Smith and the Kid, and even now I didn't know what we would do. We'd be shot down the minute we went through the front door, if we attempted to go after Landon and his bunch in the hotel. All the old men in town wouldn't be able to help Kate if that happened.

They were all staring at me as if believing I had some dead sure solution to the problem. Finally the Kid asked bluntly: "What are your plans, Del?"

I had to admit I didn't have any. "It's a stand-off, I guess."

"Then I'll fix it," the Kid said, and started toward the back door.

"Where the hell are you going?" I yelled.

He turned just before he reached the back door. "You stay out of it until it's time for you to make your play. You'll have your chance. I'm aiming to flush our rabbits out of their hole."

"Don't go over there!" I said, and realized I was still yelling at him. "It's my responsibility, and I don't aim for you to get beefed doing my job."

"It ain't your job any more'n it's mine or John's," the Kid said. "It was that way from the minute Kate hired the three of us. I know what I'm doing. They know you. They don't know me."

He wheeled back toward the door, opened it, and stepped out into the alley, shutting the door behind him.

# Chapter Twenty-Four

All I could do was to stand there and silently curse the Kid for taking this on himself. No matter what he'd said, I still felt that it was basically my fight and that I had brought the Kid and Smith into it. I was the one who was in love with Kate, and I was fighting for my future happiness as well as hers because I wouldn't be happy if she wasn't, and I knew she would never get over losing the Diamond M if that happened.

"Don't blame yourself, son," Smith said, giving me his lopsided grin. "I've known the Kid longer than you have, and I've learned to keep my mouth shut when he gets that wild look in his eyes. There was nothing you could do short of shooting him."

"They'll kill him!" I said, the words erupting from me in a shout of frustrated fury. "They'll kill him the minute he shows his face."

"Maybe not," Smith said. "In the first place, they don't know him. Sloan saw him eating with us in the hotel dining room, but that didn't mean he'd be backing you with his gun. In the second place, he's damned handy with his iron. I'd say he'll take Sloan."

"They'll still kill him," I said. "There's so many of them."

Smith shrugged. "I've told you before, Del. He's not like us. He was born to hang or be shot. He knows it. Sometimes he acts like he wants to get it over with."

Kate was beside me, an arm around me. "Now you know how I've been feeling. I've stayed awake every night since you saved my life that first time wishing I had never got you involved in my troubles."

"Don't wish that about me," I said. "Your troubles are my troubles."

"Thank you," she said. "That makes me feel better."

"Besides," Smith said, "when a man hires out his gun, it's the chance he takes."

"We should have gone with him," I said. "The three of us would have had a chance."

Smith shook his head. "He's got a better chance by himself. Landon would have started the ball the minute he spotted you. Surprise will give the Kid an edge."

Jessup had been standing at a window, looking across the street at the hotel. He said: "It's kind of hard to see what's going on over there, with the sun shining on the windows the way it is, but it looks to me like there's five men with rifles standing at the windows in the lobby. I suppose they're still waiting for you to come down from the judge's office."

"There should be six of them," I said.

"That's right," Smith agreed. "Six of 'em rode in while ago."

"One of them might be over at the bar," Jessup suggested. "Anyhow, I only count five."

"That's one place we've got them," I said. "They don't know how long we were staying up there in the judge's office. The longer they wait, the more nervous they're going to get."

"Sooner or later they'll break," Smith said. "Men like Landon are never much on waiting when they've got the advantage of numbers. Sooner or later he'll send Sloan up the stairs to see what's holding you."

"Or they'll start firing at the judge's windows," Jessup said bitterly. "Landon will be happy if the judge is killed.

He knows what the judge thinks of him." He took a long breath and glanced at Kate. "This town will never be the same after today, and we thank you for it. We've been hating ourselves for a long time, kowtowing to Max the way we have. Now we'll start living, or we'll be dead. Either way is better than it has been."

Jessup continued to stand by the window, the rest of us remaining ten feet or more back of him so Landon and his men would not see us. The waiting seemed to go on and on. The mangy black dog that had been sleeping in the dust in front of the livery stable woke up, stretched, yawned, scratched himself, then got up and ambled down the street. I was surprised to see how long his shadow was. Time had gotten away from me, and it was later than I had thought. It seemed to me that the Kid was taking a long time to do whatever he figured on doing, and impatience began to goad me.

"You think they nailed the Kid?" I asked.

We were silent as we waited, each minute seeming to drag out for more than its allotted sixty seconds. I felt my nerves tightening, knowing that, if Landon's men had caught the Kid, Smith and I would have to get him out regardless of the odds.

If I judged Landon right, he'd be the kind to torture a man to make him tell what he knew. Not that the Kid knew anything of importance, but Landon wouldn't know that. In my mind I rated Landon as a white Apache and gave him credit for knowing all their tricks.

Then it came, crashing into my consciousness even though I had been expecting something to happen, two shots slamming into the silence so close together that the second seemed to be an echo of the first. I started toward the door, but Smith grabbed my arm.

"Hold it," he said. "You're inclined to go off half-cocked. Give the Kid a little time before we count him out."

I hesitated, glancing at Kate. She nodded as if agreeing with Smith. I knew they were right, that I might be committing suicide if the Kid was down, but I still couldn't see the right way to play the cards.

"They're coming out," Jessup said as if he couldn't believe it. "By golly, that gunslinger friend of yours dealt himself a winning hand."

All three of us crowded against a window, not caring now whether Landon saw us or not. Landon came out, then three others followed. I didn't recognize any of them except Landon, but I did notice that Hawk Sloan was not among them. Then I noticed something else. Landon was the only one of the four who was carrying a gun.

The Kid was the last men through the door. He yelled: "Here's your pigeon, Del!" He stopped as soon as he stepped off the boardwalk and leaned against one of the posts that held up a corner of the roof that shaded the porch of the hotel. He held his gun rock-steady in his right hand as he ordered: "Landon, you stop right there. The rest of you bust the breeze getting out of here."

Smith and I were out of the bank by then, standing in the middle of the street. Landon had stopped and was staring at me, a very frightened man, I thought, if the tic throbbing rhythmically in his cheek was any indication of his feelings. Still, I sensed that the bravado and sheer arrogance that had been so apparent in the man were still there.

Landon's cowhands mounted and galloped out of town. Still, Landon stood facing me, waiting and saying nothing, his right hand close to the butt of his gun. I moved toward him, but he began backing away.

I shot a quick glance at the Kid and saw that he was still

leaning against the post, but now the gun was beginning to sag in his hand. I realized he had been hit, but I had no idea how bad off he was because I had to keep my eyes on Landon. I didn't know if he was going to draw or not. I was sure he had not expected the situation to end up this way, and I was equally sure he didn't want to fight, but he was cornered, and he had no way out except to run. I didn't look for him to do that. His reputation would be ruined if he did.

"You said I wouldn't leave here alive," I said. "Go ahead and make your play, and we'll see who's still alive to leave town."

He backed up another step, glancing toward the hotel roof, and suddenly it struck me that six men had ridden into town. The Kid must have got Sloan, so five men should have come out of the hotel. One was unaccounted for. I started to lift my gaze to the hotel roof, realizing I was an easy target for the man who was up there, but in that instant a rifle cracked behind me from somewhere along the street. A moment later a man tumbled off the hotel roof to fall like a sack of beans into the vacant lot between the hotel and the next building.

Landon stood frozen, and suddenly the arrogance that had been so much a part of him was gone. His mouth sagged open in sheer astonishment as if this was something he could not believe had happened. He was not one to leave anything to chance, but now what had been his ace in the hole was gone.

Landon wheeled and started to run, his back a tempting target. I had been geared to go for my gun. I wanted to kill him because of his attempts on Kate's life, but also because, as long as he was alive, Kate would have no peace.

Now I could only stare in absolute amazement. I thought

that he would stand and fight like any cornered rat, and here he was, plunging away from me as if certain I would not shoot him in the back.

I yelled: "Landon!"

The sound of my own voice beat against my ears. I was surprised to hear it because I had not consciously yelled at him. I'm not sure what went through his mind, but he must have realized that, if he wanted to stay in this community, this was the one thing he could not afford to do.

Whatever his reasoning, Landon stopped as suddenly as he had started. He whirled, sweeping his gun up from leather. He got in one quick shot and missed, not by much, because I felt the slug tug at my shirt just above my right shoulder, but enough.

I drew my gun, probably the fastest draw I had ever made in my life, and fired. He was jolted back a full step as he pulled the trigger the second time, a wild shot that must have gone ten feet over my head. I fired again, although I knew it was a waste of lead. He was down, sprawled in the dust of the street, gun falling from slack fingers, his hat knocked off his head to lie beside him.

I paced toward him slowly, not sure if he was capable of lifting his gun and firing at me again, but, when I reached him, I knew he would never lift a gun again, never hire a paid killer again. I felt no remorse about killing him, no sympathy for this man who had been raised as Kate's brother, but had not felt any brotherly affection for her. Only jealousy, perhaps hurt feelings because she had refused to marry him, but, most of all, sheer greed for a fortune that was not legally his as long as Kate was alive.

Suddenly I remembered the Kid. I holstered my Colt and turned toward the hotel porch, and, as I turned, I saw Charley Nathrop standing in the street, a rifle in his hands.

So it was the preacher who had shot Landon's dry-gulcher off the hotel roof.

The Kid was down, lying on his back within three feet of the hotel porch, a bright red splotch spreading across his chest. Smith had reached him before I had and was kneeling on one side of his motionless body. At first I thought he was dead, and I realized with amazement that he had been fatally shot inside the hotel, but he had stayed on his feet long enough to force Landon into the street and to drive his crew out of town.

Then the Kid opened his eyes. He knew he was dying, I thought, but I saw no fear or regret in his eyes. He grinned a little, tried to lift a hand but could not. He said in a voice so faint I hardly heard it: "Sloan drew on me. I had my gun in my hand, but he was so damn' fast. I nailed him, but not in time."

I was so choked up I couldn't say anything for a few seconds, then I managed: "Thanks, Kid. You did a job."

"I done what I figured on doing," he breathed.

I picked up his hand that was nearest to me and held it. He did not try to pull it back, but gave it a faint squeeze as he said: "Good riding, Del. You, too, John. You always said I was born to hang or be shot. I'm glad I'm not hanging."

Then he was gone. I wiped the back of my hand across my eyes and saw that tears were running down Smith's cheeks. We got to our feet, only then noticing that a dozen men surrounded us. One was the doctor who made a quick check of the Kid's body and rose and said: "He's dead." It was, I thought, the most unnecessary remark I had ever heard in my life.

I saw Nathrop in the circle of men and extended a hand to him. I said: "I've got you to thank for being alive. I sure didn't see that gent on the roof, and, if I had, I couldn't have taken time to shoot him. Landon would have plugged me if I had."

"I'm glad to be of some service, my friend," he said. "You don't fully understand yet, but, if you stay here, and I think you will, you'll realize that you have done all of us a favor."

"I sure wasn't any help," Smith said bitterly. "I was watching Landon and never thought about him having a man on the roof."

Some men were carrying the Kid's body away as I turned to see Kate standing in front of the bank. I hurried to her, and, when she saw me coming, she ran to me, and we met in the middle of the street. We hugged each other, not caring who saw us or what they thought about the spectacle we were making.

It was kind of crazy, but in those few seconds a lot of memories rushed through my mind: of how I happened to leave home, to come here, to have been in the hotel at just the exact right second to save Kate's life. Someday I would talk to Nathrop about it.

When we broke apart, we walked toward the bank, our arms around each other. Nathrop caught up with us. Smiling, he said: "There's nothing like trying to drum up a job, is there? I hope I will have the privilege of. . . ."

"Oh, you will, Reverend Nathrop," Kate said. "Tomorrow. Or the day after. I don't want to wait. You see, I belong to this man."

I wasn't irritated by her saying that this time. It worked both ways, so I said: "I belong to her as much as she belongs to me. She's right. We don't want to wait."

Smith was walking beside us, looking smug as if this was what he had expected. He said: "I've been having some crazy notions lately. I think I'll go back home and face the music. It'll be better than running, no matter which way it goes."

"I'll borrow enough from the bank to pay you what I owe you," Kate said. "It will take some time, I suppose, to unravel all the red tape before Daddy's estate is settled." She stopped just before we reached the front door of the bank. "I'm so sorry about the Kid. I wish I could thank all three of you properly."

"Working for you is thanks enough for me," Smith said. "I learned a lot these last weeks from you, mostly about courage."

"We've all learned something," I said.

Kate nodded gravely. "I'm sure I did. Now we've got to learn how to run a ranch, although I'm going to unload most of the responsibility onto my foreman. He can't get out of it just because he's my husband."

Smith grinned. "Now you see what it's going to be like to be a husband."

"Why," I said, "it's a punishment I'll be happy to take."

**Wayne D. Overholser** has won three Golden Spur awards from the Western Writers of America and has a long list of fine Western titles to his credit. He was born in Pomeroy, Washington, and attended the University of Montana, University of Oregon, and the University of Southern California before becoming a public school teacher and principal in various Oregon communities. He began writing for Western pulp magazines in 1936 and within a couple of years was a regular contributor to Street & Smith's *Western Story* and Fiction House's *Lariat Story Magazine*. *Buckaroo's Code* (1948) was his first Western novel and remains one of his best. In the 1950s and 1960s, having retired from academic work to concentrate on writing, he would publish as many as four books a year under his own name or a pseudonym, most prominently as Joseph Wayne. *The Bitter Night, The Lone Deputy,* and *The Violent Land* are among the finest of the early Overholser titles. He was asked by William MacLeod Raine, that dean among Western writers, to complete his last novel after Raine's death. Some of Overholser's most rewarding novels were actually collaborations with other Western writers: *Colorado Gold* with Chad Merriman and *Showdown at Stony Creek* with Lewis B. Patten. Overholser's Western novels, no matter under what name they have been published, are based on a solid knowledge of the history and customs of the American frontier West, particularly when set in his two favorite Western states, Oregon and Colorado. When it comes to his characters, he writes with skill, an uncommon sensitivity, and a consistently vivid and accurate vision of a way of life unique in human history.